I0539642

Another Left Shoe

an anthology

BLUE DRAGON PRESS
MARYLAND

Includes illustrations by Keyser Söze, Debra Eloise, Alison Piotrowski, and Betsy Riley -- used with permission. All illustration remain the property of the creators.

Blue Dragon Press

ISBN-13: 978-1-62220-019-1 (POD version)

Dan Marvin

Another Left Shoe

an anthology

compiled & edited by
Betsy A. Riley

Table of Contents

 **Dan Marvin** writes from his South Florida estate. His stories have appeared in many online publications including *eFiction*, *Short Humor*, *AlienSkin*, *Golden Visions*, and many more. He also has written **Briefs for The Reading Room** (an anthology of one-page stories) and a sequel called **Change of Briefs**.

For more about Dan's writing, visit
<u>DanMarvin.wordpress.com</u>

Left Shoe OCD

Dan Marvin

Fourteen... fifteen... sixteen. Sixteen? Steven James had walked this staircase every day for 14 years, always starting on his left foot, and every day for 14 years there had been exactly 15 stairs. Just as there were always 53 steps between the front door and this staircase, 27 of them left steps and 26 right. Today, however, there were 27 left steps as always, but 27 right steps too. That could potentially be explained by having to step over a bum sprawled at the entrance to the platform, but sixteen steps on the stairs could not.

All of his life, Steven James had been told he was not right. The little rituals he did to get his morning started, not right. The constant flipping of the light switch, up and down 10 times, then one for good measure, not right. The maddening desire to go back and make sure he had locked the door even though he knew he had locked the door. Not right. And the counting, always counting, that was definitely not right. Except today there was one extra stair. Who else would know that?

When he got home from work, he sat down at the computer keyboard and dashed off a quick note to his OCD support group. Did anyone else find something strange today? In short order he was getting replies from all over the planet saying that yes, the wallpaper had one more flower pattern this morning and the sidewalk had an extra square and the carpet was one step wider. Steven James was on to something, something big, but what?

***

Dr. Miposian sat across the oak desk, letting Steven finish with all of the details. The stairs and the platform and the wallpaper and even something about how long it took a toilet to flush in Jakarta. "Well Steven, what do you think it all means?" The psychiatrist asked.

"I have no idea, I can't for the life of me figure out how it all ties together. It's like the entire fabric of reality is starting to expand, just a little. The exciting thing is that normal people don't see it, or if it registers at all it's a minor nuisance in their day. But for those of us that have compulsively counted our whole lives, it's too big a coincidence to ignore. Something big is going on, Dr. Miposian!"

"Steven, I'm a little disappointed in this setback. You were doing so well." The doctor clucked his tongue disapprovingly. "I'm going to increase your medication dosage, please have this prescription filled immediately."

Steven's chest deflated noticeably. "So you think I'm crazy, is that it?"

"No Steven, we never say 'crazy.' I think you just had a setback and that reality isn't really changing. If reality is the same, then you must be what has changed, don't you think?"

Steven sighed. "Yes, I suppose so. Thank you Doctor." He took the prescription from Dr. Miposian and walked out the door.

The doctor turned to a computer console behind him. His four arms typed quickly even though the Cridasian alphabet has 473 characters.

***

"Subject James has sensed the shifting of the boundaries of reality." The 'doctor' typed. "We must pay more attention to the small details if we are going to relocate the Earthlings successfully. Some of them have begun to sense that the containment capsule is an imperfect replica of their world. Please advise." The cursor sat on the blank screen for a moment or two, and then the screen began to fill with instructions.

 **Eve Gaal** was inspired to be a writer when she received a toy typewriter at age four. After a college internship of feature writing for her employee newsletter, she continued working at metropolitan newspapers. After a long varied career at daily papers, she published her first novel, Penniless Hearts which is part adventure, part humorous romance and all about communication. When not writing stories or poems, Eve is chasing two rescued Chihuahuas around her backyard.

Read more about Eve at **evegaal.com**

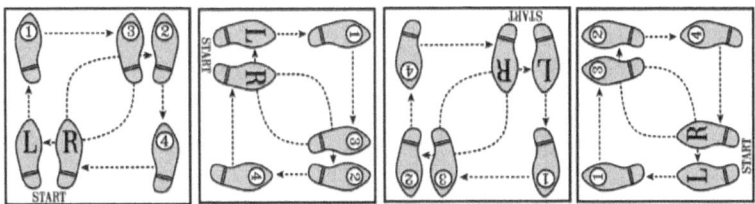

Circles and Tangos

Eve Gaal

First, they showed me the steps to the waltz while Strauss blared from the Magnavox stereo. One two three, one two three, and I'd squish my father's toes. I was a kid and it was New Year's Eve. Maybe I should clarify that I was a clumsy bookworm without rhythm. After that, there was the foxtrot—one-two and step, one-two and squash, as my dear mother laughed and gently surmised that I was born with two left feet.

Later that morning and way past my bedtime, I watched the two of them sashay across our linoleum floor and wondered about that stuff they taught me in science class about certain traits skipping a generation. They were both so graceful, and outside of the obvious physical resemblance, it seemed we didn't have much in common. I'd stare at them turning and spinning and concentrate on their polished shoes. Amid the holiday hubbub, they sparkled like angels flittering around on a cloud. Would I inherit any of their remarkable talent and organizational skills? Or would I need to worry that the circle of life had tossed my genes into a new creation, perhaps shearing off elements I wouldn't use in an ever-changing world? Snip. Snip. Snip.

Boxes labeled with color-coded cutouts filled the bottom of Mom's well-organized closet. Little circles of red paper denoted the red pumps, a pink-circled cutout on the tennis shoe box and black and navy circles graced lots of black sandals, wedges and stilettos stacked into easily accessible rows. Comfortable and practical shoes for dancing, for hiking, for walking on the boardwalk. Each had a quarter-sized cutout on the box. Her closet filled up with shoes for smelling flowers in the park, gardening, or easy-to-remove slip-ons and flats for trips to the beach. There were shoes for work that could look good with a nice skirt or a dress, and shoes that were usually only worn to church. There were special shoes for theatre events, a Sunday brunch or weddings. Hidden in the corner were aging ski boots with red laces. Dainty patent leather shoes worn once or twice were at the bottom of a stack along with a few that didn't seem to fit or were out of fashion. Pointy-toed, rounded, clogs, boots, mules ... .

Maybe someday the girls would like these, she thought, cutting out the glittery circle and taping it onto the box. She smiled thinking about the garish, five-inch gold heels that were on sale and she remembered thinking about how decadent and fancy they looked when she tried them on at the store. Over the top and yet slightly goddess-like in a statement-making Grecian style that looked magnificent with her gray wool dress and its elegant buttons. Gold paper was hard to find but she found a leftover piece of gold foil from the Easter candy rabbit and started cutting around for the circle. Snip. Snip. Snip.

Out of breath, I ran into my mother's room. "Mom, can I borrow some shoes?" I asked, hoping she had a pair to match my colorful outfit. At this point in my life, everything about me spelled creativity, spontaneous combustion, and self-absorbed teenage chaos.

"When's he coming?" she asked. She sat at her desk snipping something with those adorable little scissors from her sewing basket.

"Any minute," I responded nervously, sneaking a spray of her expensive French cologne. "I need something cool looking. Didn't you buy some cute looking wedges last summer?"

"Oh yeah, the ones that remind me of the Tango. I love those. I think they're down there on the bottom," she said, pointing towards the closet.

I looked in the closet and didn't see a box with a colorful tag. The strappy wedges were multi-colored with a wooden sole, fabric and jute ties that wound up your leg. "Tango?" I asked, with my head buried under my mother's clothes where the smell of mothballs and perfume combined with the smell of leather.

"Yes dear. Your mother used to dance the Tango like that singer. What's her name? Oh, you know-- Shakira."

"Oh wow. I'm not sure I want to think of you that way, Mom," I mumbled, ungracefully lifting myself off the carpet. "I don't see them in there. Did you put them somewhere else?" I looked in the mirror to make sure I didn't mess up my hair. Did I smudge my makeup while squirming around looking for the shoes?

"No, they're in there somewhere. I haven't got around to labeling the box. Look on the right side on the floor."

"Yup," I reached down under her clothes and down on the right side were the happy, stylish summery sandals. "Here they are," I smiled, hurriedly putting them on and vainly turning in front of her mirror.

A car horn blared in the middle of the street. "They look nice dear," she said. "Don't stay out too late."

"Thanks Mom," I yelled, running to my date. Just another date, perhaps a dance of all things.

That was many, many years ago. Pages ripped from a calendar. Painful memories like tiny circles torn from our heart. Snip. Snip. Snip.

When she had a stroke and lost the ability to walk, she sat in a wheel chair. She loved her shoes and we often spoke about how she'd get better someday, especially if she did the necessary therapy. Therapy however, was painful and she didn't see much progress. Slowly, she began giving away her shoes because she could only wear slippers or her pink tennis shoes. Sadly, she never even looked in her closet anymore. Many of her shoes didn't fit me but those wild looking multicolored sandals with the four-inch wedges are now in my closet next to some of those old shoeboxes with the faded cutouts. A connection to something I didn't inherit. Like the ability to dance.

I hope my mother forgives me for not kissing her goodbye. I hope she can walk next to the shore and smell the flowers in Heaven. I hope she can go barefoot if she wants to—but more than anything else—I hope she can dance the Tango.

These are the actual shoes from the story.

 **Laura Rittenhouse**, born in the US, now calls Australia home. Her career in IT gave her the opportunity to live and work in six different countries on five different continents and, while rewarding, just wasn't how she wanted to spend her days. In 2006 she gave up that career to focus on her passion, writing.

Laura's first novel, *Starting Over*, was published in 2009 and is available in both electronic and print formats. Two more novels are complete, but, as yet, unpublished. She's also finished a non-fiction travel book, which offers the reader an amusing account of her recent eight-month camping trip in Australia's Outback. In between writing books she occasionally writes short stories in a variety of genres, several of which have been published in a variety of media.

When Laura's not writing, she can be found wandering the 18-acre farm she shares with her chickens, her dog, her cat, over half-a-million honey bees and, of course, her husband.

For more about Laura's writing, visit
www.laurarittenhouse.com

Left for Dead

Laura Rittenhouse

The flight attendant didn't even notice that he'd bumped Maggie's seat as he bent to pick up a pillow in the aisle. Still, that gentle nudge was enough to pull her out of a surprisingly deep sleep. She looked around the cabin and spotted the *fasten seat belt* sign which told her the plane was finally landing.

Maggie kicked her backpack aside and poked around with her toes, feeling for her shoes. Her right shoe slid easily onto her foot but the left one was MIA. In a maneuver that made her happy she kept up her yoga even when travelling, Maggie twisted her torso and groped around what the airline's marketing department unashamedly proclaimed as "spacious legroom". Still nothing.

The same flight attendant whose pillow gathering had wakened Maggie squatted down in the aisle and asked, "Anything I can help you with?"

How embarrassing, Maggie was having a conversation with the best-looking guy she'd met in a couple of years and she was about to proclaim that she'd lost her left shoe. Nope, no way was it possible to squeeze a pick-up line or double entendre into this answer. "Um, I'm not sure. I can't seem to find one of my shoes." Maggie tucked her naked foot under her seat as she sat up, suddenly remembering it had been a while since she'd bothered with a pedicure – like a decade.

"Oh, sorry, that was me. It had wandered into the aisle so I snuck it into your backpack. It was unzipped and I figured you'd see it when you woke up."

More embarrassment followed as Maggie tugged the edge of her backpack that promptly and unceremoniously disgorged the wayward black pump. With her swollen foot halfway in the now-tight shoe, she raised her eyes to meet the sparkling blue pools of her rescuer. A sweet smile and flirty thanks were forming on her lips as she caught sight of him four rows up, helping a very short Asian man stow his carry-on in the overhead locker. She sighed realizing there'd be no chance for her to try out her best pick-up line or a witty double entendre on this flight.

In the taxi, her phone rang and Maggie spent most of the ride to the hotel getting confirmation of the maximum discount she could offer her customer. This company was actually just a prospect but Maggie liked to think of them as the customer that would help her blow away her sales target and get that bonus she'd already spent at least three times. First, she'd buy a new car – her car was a bomb and it would be lucky if the scrap yard would take it. Second, she'd book that trip to Paris she'd promised herself five years ago. Third, she'd pay off her credit cards – all four of them. She reached down to tug at the side of her left shoe – maybe she could manage to buy a new pair of practical work shoes with her windfall as well. The pair she had on were expensive and should have been something she could wear on a morning flight, stand up in all day while giving her winning presentation and go on to party in all night long without undue pain. Should have been, but weren't.

Traffic wasn't bad so she had a full hour to sit and relax in her room before it was time to walk to her customer's offices for her presentation. She kicked off her shoes, the left one took an extra flick because it had fused to her swollen foot, and turned on CNN. Nothing put her life in perspective like some depressing world news.

Fifty-five minutes later Maggie's head snapped up at the sound of an ambulance down at street level whirring past. Rubbing her neck, she promised herself no more late-night proposal work before an early flight. She stepped into her right shoe and glanced around for her left one. Unbelievably, that torture device had taken a stroll without her. She had a good mind to put on the hotel complimentary slippers and leave that dumb shoe wherever it had wandered. Then she remembered the many ways she was going to spend her bonus and dropped to her knees, finding her wayward footwear just under the edge of the couch.

The customer loved her presentation. Maggie had the answer to every question and only referred to her backup material once. If it hadn't been for her fidgeting because of the pain in her swollen left foot, she'd have been the ideal sales rep. She could already taste that French Champagne, sipped while seated on the banks of the Seine, as she and her new best client piled into a taxi heading to the restaurant where the deal would be sealed.

Several hours later she was deaf and crippled. If this idiot insisted on one more nightclub she'd rip up the unsigned contract and beat him with it until he agreed to trade shoes with her. The only consolations at this point were the free (cheap, domestic) wine she was drinking and the fact that just her right foot throbbed, the left one had lost all feeling two hours earlier.

***

When her boss called her into his office, Maggie tried not to hobble. It was important to her to always to look professional and these shoes, no matter how much the left one killed her, screamed success. Or not. Her boss had just received the news that Maggie lost the deal. She didn't hear much after that because she didn't want to know. To distract herself she scrunched her toes and focused on the physical pain while her mind ran through her finances.

There was an awkward silence and Maggie figured she'd missed something. A glance at her boss told her she'd missed him standing up to close the meeting and chase her out of his office. As she limped out, no longer trying to hide her discomfort, she visualized her old bomb driving into the base of the Eiffel Tower consuming both in a huge fireball.

***

It wasn't Paris, but a week at the coast wasn't such a bad vacation either. And her car might be a bomb, but the radio worked. Maggie sang along, optimism washing over her in waves, as she pictured herself at tomorrow's job interview, dazzling the CEO of the company based just two blocks from the surf beach. The job was perfect for her and, doubtless, her future boss would see what an asset she'd be to the firm. She smiled imagining the reaction of her future employer if he somehow caught sight of the backseat of her car. Her natural organizational skills were on display for all the world to see; an open-top bag with overflowing clothes and shoes spilled across her boogie board with her cute little dog, Belle, nestling in the middle of it all. She would definitely unpack her car before putting on her power suit and driving to her interview.

Belle loved car trips and Maggie loved the company. She'd been surprised how easy it was to find a hotel that accepted pets. The extra pet-deposit she paid didn't concern her since Belle never damaged anything other than her chew-toys. Besides, money soon wouldn't be a problem, this job she was about to land paid 20% more than the one she was about to quit.

Maggie saw Belle climb up onto the arm of the door in the back seat out of the corner of her eye. She looked in the side mirror just in time to watch Belle drop that beautiful, professional, pinching, tormentor of a left shoe out the window. It bounced onto the gravel at the shoulder and Maggie stuck her arm out of the car to wave it a relieved goodbye. Any company with offices so near the beach would be happy to hire someone who came to their job interview wearing sandals. As far as Maggie was concerned, that one left shoe could rot where it landed.

 **Annaliese Harris** began writing short fiction and adventure scenarios for her friends' role playing games in the mid 1980s. She went on to write Music and Dance Reviews for *Habibi; A Journal for Lovers of Middle Eastern Dance & Arts*, published by Shareen El Safy in Santa Barbara, CA. She also wrote *The Traveler's Journal, Ethnic Music and Dance*, experiences from her travels through Italy, Germany, England and Egypt - published in *Jareeda International Middle Eastern Dance Magazine* that is owned and edited by Mezdulene in Sutherlin, OR. Currently she enjoys writing children's stories inspired by Theodor "Dr. Seuss" Geisel and Sheldon Allan "Shel" Silverstein.

The Story of Mr. Troll
Annaliese Harris

Once there was a Mole Troll,
      who lived inside a mole hole,
      alongside of an old discarded shoe.

He collected bottle caps,
      moldy bread and ginger snaps;
      all kept next to a kettle full of goo.

Deep inside the mole hole,
      the home of Mr. Mole Troll,
      is a tidy place that's clean and neat.

There are root chairs and pillow plants,
      a garden full of farming ants;
      and a great hall where all his neighbors meet.

But who IS Mr. Mole Troll?
      And WHY live in a mole hole?
It seems so strange to those who live outside.

Is he odd, or is he scary,
　　　　just because his hands are hairy?
Why is it that this Mr. Troll must hide?

Just try coming out at night, and
　　　　you must PROMISE not to frighten--
Look and listen, unafraid of what you find...

You could catch a glimpse and see,
　　　　he's much the same as you or me.
For Mr. Troll is gentle and he's kind.

A crossing guard for snails and slugs,
　　　　he rescues drowning ladybugs
(keeping them under toadstools 'till they're dry).

He conducts a cricket choir,
　　　　frees the bunnies caught in wire,
　　　　and helps lost baby birds learn how to fly.

So if you see a mole hole,
　　　　or ANY home of any Troll,
Please don't be mean, remember, it's OK.
　　　　It's OK that he's a troll.
　　　　He is happy in his hole.
Don't disturb him, just go along your way.

The world is filled with magic bright,
　　　　both in the day and night,
　　　　for those who know to treat it all with care.

There are wonders you may find,
      if you keep kindness in your mind, when
      looking for the fairy, sprite, or gnome.

A dragonfly could be your friend,
      the firefly's light he'll gladly lend,
      to help you seek those things
      which most don't see.

But, if you spy an abandoned shoe,
      there's one thing you must not do,
      DO NOT take it,
      for it could be someone's home.

 **Sara Van der Wansem** was born in Mexico City. Her primary language is Spanish. She enjoys writing memoirs, short stories, and poetry. She has contributed monthly articles to a local bilingual newspaper in Moultrie, GA, where she was a successful administrator of a Migrant Head Start Center. Sara is retired and enjoys making dolls. She has a large collection of dolls and clowns. She is a member of several writing and poetry groups. Sara's education includes graduation from: *Instituto Mexicano Norteamericano de Relaciones Culturales*, Mexico; At Home Professions Medical Language and Transcription, Fort Collins, CO; and studies in Early Childhood Education Caregiver.

Bear and the Fancy Shoe
Sara Van der Wansem

Sleep didn't come, even if I kept very quiet. What was bothering me so much? Obviously it was the upcoming wedding of my lovely daughter Doreen. Tomorrow was the wedding. My thoughts were racing. Was he the right person for my only child? Daniel was a rough and outspoken guy, always smiling, but with a cynical look in his eyes. He looked manly in his jeans and sleeveless T-shirts. He was aware of all the women watching him with hungry eyes. He pretended not to see them, but deep down he was pleased with himself.

Doreen, my daughter, was and is a very pretty girl, with a serene beauty, always calm and self-possessed. Nobody knew she was insecure. Was she going to succeed this time? Her previous marriage to Mark, who unfortunately acted just like Daniel, was a failure -- it lasted less than a year. It took her a while after that bitter divorce to start dating again.

I was surprised when one day she came in looking so happy, and introduced me to the new man in her life. Naturally I disliked him

25

immediately, but I knew it was better to keep my thoughts to myself.

After a few hours of a restless night I was awakened by Bear, my newly acquired pet, a pretty Labrador who needed lots of training. I let him out so he could run in our big fenced yard.

There was no need to go back to bed. After enjoying a delicious cup of coffee I started putting on the bed my dress and all the accessories I was going to wear to the wedding. My dress was simple but elegant, with some small pearls sewn close to the neckline. I loved the light cream color of the satin fabric. A nice simple head ornament with some pearls (obviously) and my Gucci designer's shoes which matched the dress color. A small brooch with pearls made them look exquisite. I was pleased with what I saw.

Bear was crying outside the screen door; he wanted to get in. I let him in. Happily he ran to my bedroom very fast and grabbed one of the beautiful shoes. He ran out as fast as he could through the screen door which I carelessly left open. No need to tell that I went after him. I am glad nobody saw us, a crazy half-naked woman running after a dog and yelling.

I didn't know dogs could run and chew at the same time. When he finally stopped, the brooch was gone from the shoe, the heel had deep teeth marks, and the whole shoe looked gray instead of cream. The worse part is that Bear still refused to give it back to me. Being a softy with my dogs, the only thing I could think was that Bear was a puppy and needed to be trained.

I was still short of breath when I started looking at all the shoes in my closet; there was nothing that I could use until I remembered I still had a bag of clothes and shoes to donate. After digging in the bag I found an old pair nearly the same color with a big scratch on the heel. No problem, I got a cream looking acrylic paint I had at hand, and fixed the heel.

I felt chills all of a sudden, was this bad sign? I shook the bad feelings off and when I was ready to go, all dressed up, I put the one shoe left on top of the trash can. It looked so pretty I felt sorry to leave it there.

The success of my daughter's marriage remains to be seen.

 **Nancy Clark Townsend** was born and raised in the Borough of Manhattan, New York City, but lived most of her life in the Lower Hudson Valley of New York State. She has always shared her home with an assortment of dogs and cats, and owned and raced several harness horses. She studied Creative Writing at Empire State College, and took courses offered by "Writer's Digest".

She has written several romance and suspense novels and is currently working on a personal memoir and an anthology of animal memoirs. She is the editor and writer for "Church Chatter" a newsletter for her church, for which she creates a Bible Word Search and Bible Acrostic. She is now retired from her work as a legal and education secretary. Nancy worked with teachers to write and produce curriculum guides for elementary and high school students. In one, she re-wrote and modernized several of Aesop's Fables.

The Spectator Pumps
Nancy Clark Townsend

"What the hell?" Diane muttered.

She had eaten breakfast, showered and was ready to dress for work in her new navy pantsuit. She bought the outfit on sale along with a white silk blouse and a fabulous pair of navy and white spectator pumps. Sunday night she laid the suit and blouse neatly over the back of the boudoir chair. The shoes were still in the shoe box next to the chair – and she was certain the lid was on it.

Now the lid lay on the floor and the box contained just one shoe.

Diane scoured the bedroom. John was her prime suspect, but he had already left for work. Her husband had this *thing* about practical jokes. She looked under the desk, under the bed, in the closet and in the master bathroom. The shoe was nowhere to be found. She would definitely give John a piece of her mind tonight.

But now it was getting late. There simply was no time to search the rest of the house. This certainly put the kibosh on wearing her new outfit.

Surely the shoe would turn up later. Quickly, Diane put on one of her favorite dresses, let Samantha, their black Lab, out into the fenced yard and drove to work.

***

"I swear on my honor I didn't hide your shoe, sweetheart. I knew you wanted to wear your new outfit to work today."

Diane glared at John, but usually he confessed once confronted. She sighed and then turned an accusing eye on her two giggling children. They obviously thought it was hilarious.

"I am *not* amused, kids! Now which one of you took my shoe? If you come clean right now that will be the end of it ... *this* time."

"Maybe the ghost took it," said Alex.

At ten he was enamored of ghosts and zombies, and he was sure there was a resident ghost in their home.

"After all," her son steadfastly insisted, "this house dates back to the early 1900s. All old houses have one or more ghosts."

"Alexander!" Diane said impatiently.

The children knew that when Mom used their full names she was really angry.

"Scout's honor, I didn't take it," Alex swore.

"Well, *one* of you did, because there *is* no ghost. *Elizabeth Ann?*"

Six-year-old Beth stopped giggling.

"I didn't take it, Mommy. Cross my heart."

"You like to play dress-up in your mother's clothes," said her father.

"Yes, but I have old shoes and dresses to do that with. Mommy just bought those shoes. I *wouldn't*!"

And now the giggles turned to tears.

Diane's anger faded quickly, and she took Beth on her lap to comfort her.

"Well, guys, before you even *think* about watching TV or playing video games, you're going to search this house from top to bottom until you find my shoe. And *that*, my dear husband, includes *you!*"

John pretended to wince when confronted with what he called *the look*.

***

"I don't know where else we could look, sweetheart," John told her later as he settled down in his recliner. "I even looked around in the basement."

Diane had finally relented and allowed the children some TV time before Beth went to bed. Alex was reading in his room. She sat on the couch with the dog asleep next to her.

"I don't know either," Diane agreed reluctantly. "It makes absolutely no sense. I could almost understand if *both* shoes were gone.... Well, not really. Even then...."

"It really *has* to be one of the kids," said John, "and I hate to say it, but my money is on Alex. He's sort of a chip off the old block."

This was true. He got a kick out of his father's practical jokes.

"But this isn't in the *least* amusing," Diane said. "The shoes were on sale and a real bargain, but they still cost money and ... well ... it's kind of a *mean* joke."

"I agree he went too far this time, but without any real proof we can't punish either of them."

"I know. But if something like this happens again, I'm going to discipline *both* of them just on general principals."

Two days later, after searching high and low herself, Diane gave up. She almost threw the shoe and the shoe box in the trash but then decided against it. Instead, she put them on her closet shelf.

Although she checked all the local stores, she couldn't find another pair she liked as much as the ones she bought that first day. Finally, she settled for a different style navy shoe and wore her new outfit to work, but the pleasure had gone out of it.

***

"Mommy, Mommy!" squealed Beth from the basement. "Come and look,"

"Just a minute, honey."

Diane started the dishwasher and went down the stairs. For an old house, the basement wasn't bad. It had high ceilings and John spent the better part of a summer finishing off one section for a rec room. There was a pool table that converted for table tennis, an extra TV with an old couch, a cabinet that held all manner of games, and a dart board.

Beth stood under the stairs with Sammie. John was planning to close it in and create a cedar-lined closet for winter coats and other woolens. It was framed out, but there was still a lot of work to do.

"What is it, honey?"

"Here's your shoe, Mommy."

"What?"

"Look."

Beth pointed and there it was – beneath the bottom step. The shoe was barely visible because it was so dark under the stairs.

"How did you find it?" Diane asked.

She squatted down to pick up the shoe. It was a bit dirty but otherwise none the worse for wear.

"I thought I saw Sammie with something in her mouth, and the cellar door was open, so I followed her down. She put *this* under there."

Beth held up a stainless steel teaspoon.

"Sammie did that?"

"Yep."

The dog lay down with her head between her paws and looked sorrowfully up at Diane.

"What's going on?" asked John as he came down the stairs followed by Alex.

"Look for yourself."

John got down on his knees and put his hand into a long narrow hole under the first step. Instead of concrete, like the rest of the floor, it was dirt. He removed a number of items, among them a feathery fishing lure, a couple of shiny plastic bracelets, some more spoons, a fork, a belt buckle, two ballpoint pens, and a ping-pong ball. Each of them remembered missing these small things over a period of time, but never anything as large as a shoe.

Suddenly they were all laughing, and instead of being angry with Sammie, Diane wrapped her arms around the dog and hugged her.

"Obviously," John said, "I'll have to pour some concrete under the step to eliminate her hiding place."

"How do we stop a dog from stealing?" asked Alex.

"We'll just have to keep an eye on her and be more careful what we leave lying around," said Diane. "It amazes me she could take the lid off the shoe box and just remove one shoe. I also don't understand *why*. What would have attracted her?"

"Probably that nice smell of new leather," said John. "I wonder how she got the spoons and fork."

"I've seen her get up on a chair when it isn't tucked under the table," said Beth.

"Well," said Alex, "I still think there's a ghost involved."

Diane took her spectator pump upstairs and cleaned it off. Then she got the shoebox from the closet and placed the shoe with its mate.

"There you go, shoes – re-paired at last."

The next day Diane finally wore the pantsuit and spectator pumps to work. At lunch she told her laughing co-workers the tale of Samantha the Kleptomaniac Dog.

 **Ronnie Dauber** is a Canadian published author who enjoys writing novels that captivate the reader. She has written four of the five adventure books planned in her *Sarah Davies* series, one adult suspense-thriller and one Inspirational book. She is currently writing her second Inspirational book and plans to have it released in the summer of 2014 along with the last book in her series. Ronnie lives in Ontario, Canada with her husband and children.

The Search
Ronnie Dauber

Amy's heart pounded with anxiety as she stormed out of the classroom with her friend Brady trailing behind her. He caught up with her and walked at her side as she headed for her little gray Honda.

"Oh, Brady, where am I going to get a feature story in two days? If I don't have one to hand in on Monday, I'm going to fail and then I'm out of journalism school."

Brady shifted his backpack as he opened the driver's door for her.

"Let's go over to the diner and have some lunch. Maybe we can pick up a newspaper and just skim through it to find a story that we can follow. There has to be something there that will make a good feature story for you."

A few minutes later they were at a booth waiting for their lunch and Amy had the day's newspaper spread open on the table as she turned page after page.

"Nothing. I don't see anything that catches my eye to write about. A comet coming close to earth? Forget it; I have no interest and I'd only kill the story if I tried. Okay, here's one, 'Drive-thru coffee is on the rise in America.'"

"Sure Ames, that will put you to the head of the class."

"I know. I need something dynamic like a kidnapping or an unsolved murder."

"Well, that would certainly get Mrs. Stifflip's attention."

Amy chuckled at Brad's descriptive name for her disgruntled journalism teacher, and then suggested they finish eating and go for a drive; hopefully, they could see something along the way that would make a good story for her. They walked across the small parking lot and as Amy was about to open her car door, she spotted something red on the side of the road. She told Brady she'd be right back and then ran to it.

"Nice shoe. Too bad there's only one. I wonder who would leave an expensive shoe like this behind. I guess I should give this to the manager so she can...."

Just then, a small crinkled napkin fell out of the shoe and onto the ground. Amy quickly scooped up the napkin and opened it so she could read what was scribbled on the back.

> *Help me. Viking guy will kill me. Today is...*

Icy shivers crept across her neck as she read the note again. Was this for real? She brushed her long dark hair off of her face and looked around, but didn't see any visible evidence that a trauma had taken place. Quickly, she shoved the shoe into her oversized bag and stuffed the note in her pocket. As discretely as she could, she hustled back to the car to show Brady.

"Well, I guess the upside of this, Ames, is that this could be your feature story. We can hunt around and try to find who wrote this note and maybe even save her from this Viking guy. You can call it *One Red Shoe*. Come on, I'll help you. This could be fun."

Amy was a little annoyed that Brady always had to turn everything into something that was fun instead of taking this as serious as she did.

"This isn't funny, Brady. This poor girl could be in real danger, you know. It might not turn out to be a fun thing for us, either, especially if we stumble onto what's really going on. I mean, this could lead to something horribly bad. What if we run into this Viking guy? He could be really dangerous."

"But it could also give you your feature story, Ames, and it might even save this girl's life. So, what are we waiting for?"

"You're right. If I'm going to be a journalist then I can't let anything scare me off. Let's do it."

She sat behind the wheel and had that investigative twinkle in her eye as she smiled at Brady.

"You remember my cousin, Derrick? He's a forensic coroner at a place about thirty minutes from here. Let's take the shoe to him and have him do some DNA testing on it and see just who it belongs to."

Brady agreed and so they took the shoe to Derrick, and then returned later that evening to discuss his findings. As they sat anxiously in the waiting room of the forensic lab, a tall, clean-shaven and bald headed man dressed in a white lab coat pushed through the glass door. Derrick walked toward them with a big smile on his face.

"Okay, we've identified the DNA and it belongs to a Deborah Wilde."

Amy shook her head and looked at Brady.

"Hmm, the name isn't familiar, but I'm sure we can look her up in the phone book or even Google her so we can find out where she lives."

Derrick snickered as he tapped his clipboard.

"Are you going to visit each one and ask if they lost a shoe? Why not just try this address? It's the one that matches her driver's license."

Amy smirked as she put her cell phone back in her bag.

"Anything else you can tell us about her, Derrick?"

"Well, there are traces of - never mind. In simple words she drinks, smokes and is diabetic. So, if she's not at this address I think you can rule out the Mennonite community."

"Thanks, Derrick. I know you went out of your way to do this for me, so thanks for your help."

***

It was late in the evening when they left the lab and returned to her car so they agreed to head out first thing in the morning. At eight o'clock the next morning Amy drove to Brady's house to pick him up, and soon they were on their way.

"Geez, Ames, I feel like the prince in Cinderella. 'Is this your shoe?' What if her feet smell? What do we do then? But worse, what if she is - you know, dead?"

Amy bit her lip as she drove up a prestigious street in the richer side of the town of Wellington. Before long they were at the address that Derrick had given them, and they stared at a large, brick luxury home with a circle driveway and huge pillars that held oversized Victorian lamps.

"This could be it. It's a rich neighborhood and she'd have to be wealthy to afford those shoes in the first place."

"Well, no wonder she was kidnapped, Ames. She's probably being held for ransom somewhere until they get this one back."

Amy rolled her eyes as she scoffed at him.

"Very funny, Brady. Anyway, here we are. Maybe we should have told the police about the shoe, what do you think?"

"We're just asking Deborah if this is her shoe. There's nothing incriminating about that."

"Yeah, if Deborah *is* here."

Amy parked the car in the driveway and took a deep breath as they walked up the stone sidewalk to the front door. She pressed the door bell and held her breath as the echoing sound of the Westminster Bells penetrated her ears. She stared at Brady and he put his arm around her and told her to stop worrying.

A few seconds later a large, gruff-looking man who could have been André the Giant's twin opened the door and stared down at them. His voice was deep and threatening.

"Yes?"

Amy was intimated by his size and his voice and couldn't speak, so Brady butted in.

"We're here to see Deborah Wilde."

"Do you have an appointment?"

Brady shuffled his feet.

"No, we don't."

"Then why are you here?"

"We have something that we'd like to give her. Well, we found something that we think is hers."

The man's voice grew louder.

"Who sent you? Who are you?"

Brady introduced Amy and him and then asked again if Deborah Wilde lived here.

"She's not in right now. Leave me whatever it is you have and I'll give it to her."

Amy cleared her throat and spoke with a loud, shaky voice.

"When will she be back? We want to give this to her ourselves."

The man looked down at her with his dark, beady eyes.

"No, it doesn't work that way. You give me what it is and I pass it on to her."

"Really! Well, it doesn't work that way with us, either. You go and get her and *we'll* give it to her."

"She's not here. Give it to me."

"Well, when will she be back? Or will she be back? Maybe something's happened to her and she's....."

Brady squeezed Amy's arm abruptly to get her to stop talking as the man stepped forward. Immediately Amy and Brady stepped backwards and her insides began to shake as the fear of Deborah's welfare became imminent to her. This certainly would make a perfect feature story - if she lived to write it.

The man stretched his huge hand out to her.

"Give it to me."

"I don't think so. We have something that belongs to her and we're going to give it only to her."

Just then, a woman's voice came from behind the giant and broke the tension.

"Eric, who's at the door?"

There were several seconds of silence as Amy held her breath and stared at the overbearing man. He didn't move; he just stared back. Amy's legs slowly turned into rubber and she couldn't move.

The woman tapped the guy's arm and he stepped to the side so Amy could see a middle-aged woman dressed in a stylish light grey suit and matching grey heels. Gold hoop earrings hung behind her short blonde hair as she smiled and introduced herself.

"I'm Deborah Wilde. And you are?"

Amy took a deep breath and returned the introduction. She looked at the woman while she spoke, but her eyes constantly jumped to the big guy beside her.

"We, well I, found something that we thought might be yours, but maybe not. Or maybe. Have you lost anything lately? You know what? I think we have the wrong house. Maybe we should just be on our way."

The woman smiled as she motioned for the man to move back.

"Please come in. And relax. What do you have that you think is mine? I hope you do have something, and this is not just some trick to hand me your script. We do have a method to our madness and you need to give any scripts through the proper channels to the office and not to me here."

What? Amy opened her bag slowly and pulled out the red shoe. The woman gasped and then laughed as she took it from Amy's hands.

"My shoe! Where did you find it? I've searched everywhere for this, and in fact, I'm having another left shoe made right now to replace this one."

"I found it on the side of the road near a small diner in Westport. There was a note inside it, too."

Deborah shook her head as she waved the shoe in front of her male friend.

"Go get my other shoe, will you, Eric? This is just too funny."

Amy and Brady looked at each other as confusion stunned them both. Amy slowly took the note from jacket pocket and handed it to Deborah.

"Did you write this?"

Deborah puffed as she grinned and took the note without looking at it.

"We were on our way back from a Dezi Cruz concert in the big city and I had to use the ladies room, so we stopped at the little diner there. It was a busy night for them, I guess, since we had to park on the road. I'd been on my feet all day, and I didn't have to look dressy anymore, so I took the shoes off to wear my sandals . I guess I dropped this one there. Thank you so much for finding it, only now I'll have two left shoes."

Amy tapped the note impatiently.

"Did you write this note? Why did you say the Viking guy was killing you? Why did you ask for help?"

Deborah and Eric both laughed, and the hardness in his face that had gripped Amy with fear earlier now faded and he looked like just an oversized, but jolly man.

"Oh, geez. I wrote this at the bar during a concert break. There was a group called the Vikings that I allowed on before Dezi Cruz, just a small warm up band for the big show. One of the guys was so spaced out that he wasn't playing his guitar in tune with anyone and he was messing up the band. I had to get him off or I could be in trouble for putting him there."

Brady grunted as he lowered his eyebrows.

"So, why did you ask for help?"

Deborah snickered as she waved the note in the air.

"I didn't want to talk out loud to my assistant so I wrote the 'help me' part because I needed her to help me get them off the stage. And then I wrote that the Viking guy was killing me. He was really awful. I fired them immediately when they were done. I was going to write that today is the last time I'll blindly hire any group before the big name bands again, but I was called backstage so I just shoved it into my bag. It must have gotten into my shoe when I was at the diner trying to stuff my shoes into my bag."

Amy huffed and then shook her head.

"So, you're not asking for help, and the Viking guy wasn't trying to hurt you -- he was just part of the band? What is it, exactly, that you do?"

"I'm the coordinator for celebrity functions in Portland. I accept new film scripts and present them for publication, plus I arrange for the big bands at the city's concert coliseum, which is where I was that night."

Amy and Brady looked at each other and then burst out laughing. A few seconds later Amy explained their suspicions and what had brought them to her house.

"So, you're going to be a journalist? Well, you certainly are bold enough and brave enough. I think you'll make a great writer, Amy. In fact, maybe I can help you get that feature story."

Amy smiled and replied excitedly.

"Thanks. That would be great, but first can I ask why your friend was so aggressive toward us?"

Deborah smiled and then Eric chuckled as he looked at her.

"Eric is working on his new movie part as a doorman for the mob. He was just practicing on you."

Amy sighed in relief and nodded as she smiled at Brady. Just then, a young maid brought Deborah a portable phone so she could receive a call. Deborah stepped into the parlor and then returned a few minutes later.

"Okay. Why don't you two come with me and we'll get that feature story for you."

Amy was thrilled and yet nervous about what feature story lay ahead for her.

"Where are we going?"

The maid returned with Deborah's red jacket, and so Deborah handed Amy the paper that she'd just written on for her to hold while she changed. Amy gasped with excitement.

Bruce Springsteen!

"I think this interview will give you a great feature story, Amy. But first, I'm going to change my shoes and wear these red ones, now that I have another left shoe."

Padma Narayanaswamy, is a script writer and a freelance journalist. She writes crossover feature scripts in English. Her scripts are women centric and are family oriented.

Besides scripts, Padma has dabbled in all genres of writing like short stories, plays and articles. She has also published a poetry manuscript titled **Straight from my Heart**.

Earlier she was an Associate Editor in Shipping Times, and a Sub-Editor in Vista Communications.

On a personal note, Padma describes herself as a middle aged woman. Her husband is retired from his career as a Manager at Indian Bank. They have two sons: the first son is a freelance graphic designer and the second son is a software engineer.

For more about Padma, see:
mandy.com/home.cfm?c=nar040

Individual Identity
Padma Narayanaswamy

The birthday party was in full swing. The dancers had taken to the floor and were swaying to the latest Hindi hit film tunes. It was a thematic party: all invitees had to include red as a major part of their outfit.

"Who is this gorgeous lady, in that red flamingo? What a beautiful outfit. She must be awfully rich to afford a *KimonO* creation."

"Hush, it is the lady itself. It is Shika, designer of the *KimonO* label."

"Great, she must be really happy to be so talented and successful"

Shika grinned to herself. She had overheard the conversation. *How wrong you are, dears. Success is not sweet if you are alone. It has to be shared*

Shika was attending the birthday party of the son of her former lover and manager, Shreedar. He had returned from US and was a CEO for another garment exports company. He had proposed to her once, but she had declined. Now it was she who missed the trip down the aisle; she was alone at the altar of success.

Shika could never understand herself, how she came to choose what she called *individual identity*. She wanted to achieve something in life. She wanted to be known as Shika, instead of being known only as somebody's daughter or somebody's wife.

A woman has no individual identity especially in Indian society. I have to change it, she mused. This thought kept on harping at her, giving her no peace. *Why does this thought keep on hampering me?* she brooded.

She knew many people would give their right hand to be in her position. Her father was a scion of society with an impeccable industrial pedigree. His forefathers were the pioneers of shoe manufacturing units in the state.

***

The British were ruling the Madras presidency at that time, and were not allowing local traders to start any new units. They feared that once the Indians tasted success, the hold of the British would lessen until they lost their supremacy in India.

After the *Quit India* movement, the British allowed the local people to undertake industrial activities on their own initiative. It was during this period

that Shika's forefathers started a shoe-manufacturing unit. The story of how her great grandfather Mr. Siva Subramanian started the shoe industry was a legend by itself.

The family member of a Governor lost her shoe while she was climbing the tram. The party could not find a pair anywhere, so they approached Shika's grandfather, who was a trader.

He took the shoe to his cobbler and made a new pair. The family was impressed and offered a lot of money in payment. The profit made her great-grandfather ponder, and he soon established the first shoe industry in India

Sivakami was his child bride of thirteen. Siva Subramanian was in his early forties. He had earlier marital relationships but had lost his two wives due to childbirth and illness. He married Sivakami for progeny. Sivakami was at a loss, herself. She did not understand what marriage was about. Siva Subramanian patiently taught her how to run the family and how to look after his needs. Above all he taught her how to love him. Sivakami gave birth to three children (two girls and a son).

Siva Subramanian celebrated the birth of his son with great pomp and fanfare. *Pandals* were constructed. *Homams* were conducted, *dhanams* were given to poor Brahmins and Vedic mantras were chanted to increase the lifespan of the child.

Many eminent artists were asked to grace and sing for the occasion.

Siva Subramanian was a satisfied man. Now he had everything: wealth and an heir, but fates are not kind. How can man stay happy? Just when he was planning to celebrate his *Sashtiyabthapoorthi* he died asleep.

Sivakami was just twenty-four when she was widowed. She had three kids and a family business to run. In those days a widow had to shave her head and wear white garments. Sivakami did not give in to social pressure. She got herself educated with the help of a tutor and passed the exams privately. She then tried to learn the rope of her husband's business.

People tried to cheat her thinking that she was a woman and would not know. She however taught them a lesson. She appointed able and honest persons to guide her in the business. Soon she started earning profits even more than her husband.

***

All these stories must have affected me, thought Shika. She was proud of her great-grandmother and decided to follow in her footsteps.

Many suitors came in asking for Shika's hand. She was beautiful, rich and intelligent. What more could a man require in his fiancée? She politely refused.

"No marriage for me, unless I am someone or something of my own," she stormed at her mother. Her father smiled indulgently.

Her mother lost her cool, "Instead of advising her he encourages her. It is as if I am only a stupid creature who is always grumbling at her."

"Another Sivakami in the making. Her *Kollupatti* (great-grandmother) was ahead of her time; let Shika go with the times," laughed her father.

Shika had a keen dress sense. She had modeled some clothes for an advertising company, but it was not her cup of tea.

Who would want to be a clothes horse? she thought to herself, *The best thing is designing clothes for the models.*

***

Once she had decided the course of action, she enrolled in a full five-year fashion-designing course. She graduated with flying colors and finished the course with a top ranking.

Next Shika went to London, where she worked under a famous British designer. It was from him she learnt to pay heed to the most minute details about operating a boutique. How can a creation be functional and aesthetic too? How could one juxtapose the artful, precise minimalism of Japanese yen to the decadent extremes of a period

French boudoir, to the dazzling array of color and reflection of Indian *sheeshmahal*? She learned that the architectural elegance and location of the store also affect sales.

Job offers poured in from both the big players and small players in the world of haute couture. Shika chose to become the manager of a small division in a quality firm. Many were surprised at the move, but she felt that she would be able to make independent decisions. In the long run, she was certain it would help her career.

Shika never restricted herself to being only a manager. She worked as a merchandiser, designer, and even as a saleslady. She learned the nuances of her division with so much enthusiasm that the boss made her a partner in the firm.

Shika located her *Cool and Comfort Designer House* in Anna Salai, the business hub of the city. *Cool and Comfort* was luxurious. High ceilings, onyx flooring, plush carpeting, and mirrored corridors gave an aura of majestic space to the store. Strategic lightening enhanced the colors of the clothing. At the center, in the inner sanctum, there was a unique couture room. An antique chandelier painted with lotuses, and a gargantuan modern-day *sheeshmahal* ceiling reflected light to create dazzling mosaic patterns in the room. It had an ambience of calmness and quiet grandeur.

At first Shika catered to a small clientele. Slowly, she broadened her business. The next step was to export her labels. "Shika gossamer" was a collection of silk skirts plaited with gold and silver. Another prêt-a-porter item was labeled "exclusive Shika Ancient Culture" -- in this collection there was a blend of ancient Indian motifs with modern patterns. Shika kept on innovating. She blended the Japanese kimono with Indian elements like *ghungroos* and sequins, and labeled it as *KimonO*. These became a rage, and orders poured in. She began exporting her labels in a big way. Some of the biggest European garment houses were her clients.

Shika had achieved her dream. She was at the pinnacle of glory. What she dreamed, she had achieved. *Had this brought her peace, or happiness?* she reflected to herself.

***

It was announced that Shika was to be awarded **Designer of the Year**. She received the notification along with a request to bring some person close to her as a guest, since there was going to be a reception for her. To her dismay, Shika found that there was nobody to stand by her in her success. Her parents had long before left for their heavenly abode. Her close friends from younger days could not be present with her in her D-day, as they had their own commitments in life

"Look Shika, we cannot rush to you as before. We've all got our own families," burst out her friend when Shika chided her for not turning up.

Shika realized that she had gained nothing in her search for individuality. She had missed the bus. Sivakami, her great grandmother, was an achiever in life in the true sense. She was doing something for the family, whereas Shika has lost her way. Her individuality has killed her chances for romance.

Once Shika had fallen in love with Shreedhar, her manager. He was a product of IBM and she had hired him to help her in the business.

"Shika, you should leave the business, and come with me to the states. I cannot be your househusband." But Shika could not let go of her dream at that time.

Now, her mother's words kept on haunting her, "Marriage does not mean you lose your individuality. What you gain is companionship and a family. A truly successful woman is one who balances hearth and bacon."

What's the use of mourning my past? Shika told herself philosophically. *In life you lose something and then gain something. We cannot set back the clock. We cannot correct our past mistakes; what we can do is learn lessons from them and prevent further mistakes in the future.* She decided to put her experiences into a book, so that others could learn her lessons before it became too late for them.

Indian Wedding Dress

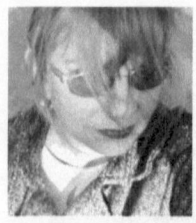 **Annaliese Harris** began writing short fiction and adventure scenarios for her friends' role playing games in the mid 1980s. She went on to write Music and Dance Reviews for *Habibi; A Journal for Lovers of Middle Eastern Dance & Arts*, published by Shareen El Safy in Santa Barbara, CA. She also wrote *The Traveler's Journal, Ethnic Music and Dance*, experiences from her travels through Italy, Germany, England and Egypt - published in *Jareeda International Middle Eastern Dance Magazine* that is owned and edited by Mezdulene in Sutherlin, OR. Currently she enjoys writing children's stories inspired by Theodor "Dr. Seuss" Geisel and Sheldon Allan "Shel" Silverstein.

Annaliese decided to rewrite an old nursery rhyme, to give it a better ending. Here's an old version:

There was an old woman who lived in a shoe.
She had so many children, that all she would do,
was give them some broth without any bread,
then whip them all soundly and put them to bed.

The Shoe on the Left
Annaliese Harris

There once was a woman,
whose home was not new.
She had many children and *knew* what to do!

She loved them COMPLETELY,
Made sure they were fed.
She read them all stories each night before bed.

The Moral (to Parents)

There are Parenting Styles
claimed to be "Tried and True";
used by that old woman who lived in a shoe.

Such abuse will not end
'till the chain is cut through
Please remember; the future depends upon you....

Timothy Hurley is a writer of short fiction and humor. He lives with his wife in Brooklyn, New York, where they both ride the subway and climb stairs, but they never run for elevators. Timothy's humorous fiction has appeared in online magazines and print anthologies.

Read more about him at **thelunaticassylum.com**.

Stoop Shoe
Timothy Hurley

On Tuesday Hailey had a disturbing dream that left her wondering about her recent move to New York. That night, as the twenty-five year old slept, she battled her bed covers like an agitated alligator. In her nocturnal vision she stood, a petite redhead in jeans and sweatshirt, on the sidewalk in front of her Brooklyn apartment building. She observed the people who passed her and studied each, looking into their eyes. None returned her gaze, and as each individual passed by without a word, her heart rate increased.

An old man drew her gaze to the end of the block, and she recognized her grandfather standing on the corner. Her arm shot up, and Hailey waved it side to side above her head. "Grampa, I miss you," she shouted.

"I miss you, too, Hailstorm." the old man called back, using her fifth grade nickname. Hailey began to run, but suddenly she was a ten-year old again and caught in a slow-motion movie. Her arms and legs pumped the air, but her feet made no progress on the pavement.

The mocking, disembodied face of her eighth grade teacher, the one she hated, appeared in front of her. "You'll never have friends," the face screeched, "you analyze everyone, and dissect everything." Hailey cringed, and the image cackled and faded away.

A pair of wingtip shoes—devoid of its human occupant—flexed beside her, lifting and slapping themselves on the concrete. They picked up speed and progressed toward her grandfather, who stood now gawking in apparent disbelief at his bare feet.

Hailey awakened several times during the night, and found herself bathed in sweat, tears and confusion. In spite of the pounding in her chest, she felt compelled to go back and finish the dream. But each time she returned, the apparition did not progress beyond her distressed grandfather hollering, "Hurry, Hailstorm, hurry. I'm here."

***

Hailey described the dream to her best friend and apartment-mate, Angie, the following morning on their way to work in Manhattan. The two stopped at a bakery, and Hailey fished a twenty-dollar bill from her wallet. "I've got breakfast," she said. She placed the bill on the counter, and ordered raisin bagels and decaffeinated coffee with skim milk.

The cashier turned and called to someone behind her, "Two wrinkled grapes and two why-bothers."

"I remember calling you Hailstorm," Angie said laughing and sliding her long brown hair behind her ear. "You came on strong—and hammered everything. But I haven't a clue what the rest of that means." The two nibbled and sipped as they walked past Grand Central Terminal. Angie snapped her thumb and second finger at the building's façade, "We've come a long way from Indiana."

Hailey nodded and pointed out it was exactly one week since they had left the security and comfort of their small town and families. "We need to get some things for the kitchen tonight," Hailey said. "I'm tired of paper plates. Even if we order in, I want real dishes."

***

That evening on their walk home from the subway station in Brooklyn, Hailey and Angie stopped at the stoop of an apartment building and inspected the castoffs they found there. Angie pawed through a pile. "There's dishes and books here. Good stuff. Do you want any of these books? Dibs on *Zombies Gone Wild.*"

Hailey searched through the plates until she found some that weren't chipped. "Free-on-stoop's fun. I like looking at other people's junk." She held up a carrot-colored teapot with brown stripes, "What idiot had that in their kitchen?"

"Shush. Someone might be listening. You're so critical."

Hailey lifted a leather shoe from the stoop. "Who put this here?" She turned the black oxford over and inspected the sole. "It isn't even scuffed. The laces are still bundled up like it was new. Someone's tossing a brand new shoe. Where's the other one?" She glanced around the stoop.

Angie stuffed books into her backpack, glanced in Hailey's direction, and snapped her fingers at the footwear. "I don't know. Why do you care? It's a man's."

Hailey tapped the leather sole against her thigh and looked at the windows of the five-story building. "I wonder which apartment it came from. I dreamed about shoes."

"So?"

"This is a left. Where's the right one?"

"Don't know and don't care." Angie hefted a load of dishes and books. "I got as much as I can carry. You coming?"

Hailey turned her attention from the windows and started through a pile of books. "I'll meet you at the apartment." After grabbing a couple of volumes and placing them on her stack of dishes, she resumed her scrutiny of the building. Angie, having walked far down the block, did not hear her when she continued. "There's something about this ... something." She laughed and rubbed the leather. "Maybe it's a magic shoe. Maybe it belongs to Prince Charming."

Her smile faded and she slapped the footwear. It could mean nothing, she thought, but then where was the other one? And why brand new? Angie was right, she decided. Better to be done with it. She placed the shoe on the third step, a couple of inches from the edge, adjusted it a bit, then turned and walked away with her dishes.

A few steps later she whirled, hurried back, and snapped up the footwear. "Why?" she growled at the oxford, brandishing it as if trying to shake some information from it. "What? What do you mean?"

She scanned the windows, her eyes darting from floor to floor. A fluffy white dog materialized at a window on the third floor, barked at her and disappeared. A white-haired man appeared in a robe on the second floor, peered down for a moment, and vanished.

Hailey pointed at the window. "Could be his! I'll bet it's the old man's."

A few minutes later, while Hailey was debating whether to buzz the apartment, the old man, dressed in a red and yellow checked shirt, reappeared in the window and glanced down. Hailey held the shoe above her head in her right hand and stabbed at it again and again with her left index finger. The old man's eyebrows went up, his hand went out, palm up, and he shrugged. Hailey poked the shoe again and then stabbed the air in the direction of the fellow. His lips spoke words she could not hear. She held the shoe against her stomach and, repeatedly thrust her cupped left hand toward the sidewalk, mouthing *come down*. The man stood at the window a moment and then left.

Hailey sat down on the stair. Presently, the front door opened and the old fellow moved awkwardly onto the landing above her, leaning hard on the crutch tucked under his left arm. His white hair, medium longish, looked as if someone had set off a firecracker in it. With one hand he rubbed his grey chin — not so much a beard as simply unshaved whiskers. In his other hand he held a Yankees baseball cap, which he placed over the thicket of hair. He moved to his right, gripped the railing and progressed down a couple of steps. "What do you want, young lady?"

From her position below the man, Hailey looked at his feet and noticed the oxford on his right foot matched the one in her lap. She saw nothing beneath his left trouser leg. "Is this your —shoe?" Hailey blurted and felt her face flush and turn warm. "Oh, I'm sorry. I didn't know."

"Know what? You called me all the way down here to ask me if that's my shoe?"

Hailey considered the possibility Angie was correct about learning to mind her own business.

"I didn't know you had a, you know, a—"

"Amputation? It's called amputation."

"Well, I took it. I mean I found it. On the stoop," Hailey said, pushing the shoe towards the man and then quickly returning it to her lap. She was certain it was his shoe. "I thought you were giving it away. I didn't mean to—"

"Didn't mean to steal it? 'Course I put it there. What do you want with it?"

Hailey recovered her poise and impertinence and straightened her back. Why indeed, she thought, should she be interested in his shoe — or him? And why would he put it on the stoop? It was useless, she thought, to anyone who wasn't the old man's mirror image. "No, it's only a *left* shoe," she said. "The right one's gone. Why—"

"'Not gone. I'm wearing it."

"Why would you give away just one shoe?"

"Why would you take just one shoe?"

"I don't know. It kind of spoke to me?"

"Oh, so you speak to shoes, do you? Do socks speak to you too? I could give you some of my socks to chat with."

"No, I don't mean 'speak.' It reminded me of something ... of someone. I don't know why. I didn't steal your shoe, and I wasn't trying to make you angry."

"What's the shoe saying now?"

Hailey studied the old man's face for clues to what he was thinking. He stared back but did not speak. She hesitated, and considered abandoning the footwear and leaving. But instead, she inhaled sharply and continued. "It says it doesn't get out of the apartment much."

The old man remained quiet for a moment, then smacked his lips and slapped the railing. "Says all that, does it? Did it tell you I put it out there 'cause, as you noticed, I don't need it, and a homeless guy picks up the shoes I leave? He says one new shoe is better than none. Did it tell you that?"

Hailey opened her mouth and thought, *I must be beet red.* "Oh—um," she said and bit her lip. She took the footwear from her lap and placed it on the stoop. "Sorry," she squeaked.

"Don't worry about it, young lady." His voice was softer now. "I was young and brash once. Maybe you weren't wrong about the 'it doesn't get out much' part. Maybe my shoe was glad to have someone to talk to."

"I just moved to New York for my job. My roommate and I were just getting stuff off the stoop. It seemed strange to see a shoe all by itself, Mister— ."

"Name's Horace. You can call me Ace. That's quite a talent you've got there — talking to shoes." He smiled and moved down a step.

"I thought it was a magic shoe." Hailey laughed. "Yeah, and that shoe was in my dream. It reminded me of someone."

"Magic too? And making appearances in your dreams? Not on Broadway?" He chuckled.

Hailey smiled. "I'm Hailey. I had a grandfather like you. Except he shaved once in a while."

"Oh, I shave. This grandfather — does he talk to shoes, too?"

Hailey clasped her hands and looked at them. "He passed away just before I moved to New York with Angie. She's my best friend."

Horace moved down to the step above Hailey and lowered himself to sit. "Oh, I'm sorry, Hailey. You must miss him."

"I do. He used to talk to me. He taught me to drink coffee. When I was little he let me dunk my toast in his coffee." Hailey's voice trailed off and she covered her mouth with her hand.

Horace grinned, and his teeth showed white against his gray whiskers. "Funny thing. I drink coffee. Love the smell. And there's a coffee place on Montague Street."

Hailey's face brightened. "I'll get you a coffee. I really didn't mean to take your shoe. I just couldn't figure it out."

"Alright about the shoe, already. Just leave it on the stoop." Horace slapped his knee. "Why don't you text your roommate, or whatever you kids do, and we'll get a coffee together. You girls can tell me all about moving to New York."

"Awesome," Hailey said, reaching into her backpack.

Horace grabbed the railing and pulled himself up. "You do that, and while we're waiting for her, I'll go shave. Then I'll tell you how I lost my foot when I was sailing with pirates."

Hailey looked up and smiled while her thumbs bounced over her phone.

Shoe Tree at Murray State University

 **Grace Gemini** is an Intuitive Spiritualist and Healer. She describes herself as a fearless Paradigm Surfer, striving to uplift others and help them to discover their true Selves. Through comparison and allegory, Grace re-interprets what we call "ancient Wisdom", using contemporary terminology, in order to help modern people understand what was really being said.

For more of her writing, visit "Aspiring to Grace; The Shaman's Journey"
http://grace-in-search-of-grace.blogspot.com/

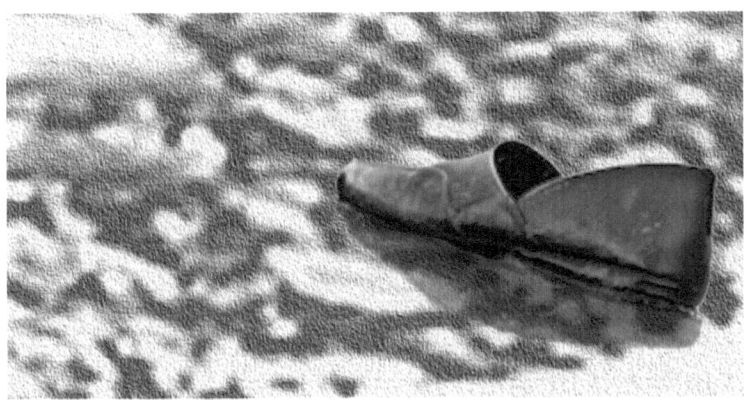

The Shoe: A Modern Fable
Grace Gemini

A little boy and his father were walking down the side of a dirt road when the child caught sight of a single shoe lying in a ditch. "Look Daddy", he said, "someone put a shoe on the side of the road. "It looked new; and try as he might the little boy could not see its mate anywhere. "Why do you suppose they left it there?" he asked his father.

The corners of the man's mouth turned up in a knowing smile. Always happy to tell a story, he began...

There once was a man who suffered from a pain in the heel of his left foot, and nothing he did would help. Looking for some relief, he went out into the courtyard of his home to talk to his wife.

His wife pursed her lips in an attitude of disdain when she heard his question and indicated that he should sit closer so that no one would overhear them.

"Nobody in our family has ever had pain like that before," she whispered. The two of them positioned themselves on a bench that sat underneath a tree that was planted in the middle of a large expanse of well-manicured grass. A few feet away, the couple's older children sat, cross-legged on silk seat cushions in two orderly rows. Their tutor moved from student to student, watching over their bent shoulders as they made neat, uniform marks on the pages of their lesson books.

The wife's gaze wandered in the other direction just across the lawn, to the youngest children, who were still too young for lessons, as they played with a ball with their nurse. "Besides, we must set a good example for our children. We wouldn't want anyone to think that this sort of thing ran in our family." She continued resolutely. "Just ignore it," she said, "it will go away in time."

So, the man tried to ignore the pain, and walked with a pronounced limp from place to place.

But his foot still hurt.

***

One day, as he slowly made his way down the road, he ran into a friend of his and decided to ask him about his problem.

"That's easy," said the man. "You need new shoes, like the ones that I am wearing." The unhappy man looked at the shoes on his friend's feet and saw that they were very fancy and expensive shoes indeed. "I have found," his friend continued, "that purchasing something new always helps me when I am feeling unwell. Have you seen our neighbor across the creek?" The man's friend looked from side to side warily, and leaned forward saying, "I mean, have you *seen* his shoes? Definitely second-rate," he whispered with a self-satisfied grin.

The man was unsure, but, if owning such an expensive pair of shoes would give him relief from the pain, it was worth the money if it helped. So he hopped into town and bought several pairs, which cost him a small fortune.

The new, expensive shoes helped for a little while, but before long, the pain returned and the man was unhappy again. This time, he was forced to walk with a cane to take the weight off his foot, and he was not pleased. He did not want to spend so much money every time his foot hurt, so he decided to visit his physician for a cure.

***

The physician was a very learned man. He had all kinds of certificates and diplomas in gilded frames hanging on his office walls. He propped the man's leg up on a stool while he considered the situation with a very serious expression on his long, bearded face. He didn't speak to the man, but every so often he would inhale sagely and say, "I see," to nobody in particular. When he was done looking he turned to the nurse and said something to her that the man did not understand.

She nodded and left the room. Several minutes later, she returned with a number of small pots. "You must apply the first one twice a day, every other day," she said to the man. "The second one, three times a day but only every third day, the third once a day every two days, and the fourth as often as you like."

Her long fingers lingered over the lids as she spoke, pointing out which pot was which. The man lifted the first pot and opened the lid. He grimaced at the terrible odor and looked at the greasy-looking ointment. He was ashamed to admit that he had already forgotten the instructions.

"What is wrong with my foot?" he asked the physician.

The physician just nodded to the nurse who answered, "We're not sure. But these ointments will ease the pain."

"What good is that?" said the man. "When the medicine is gone, I will just have to come back for more."

The nurse looked annoyed and said curtly, "The doctor knows what is best for you. Here is a crutch to help you along."

The man was still unhappy but he didn't want to argue with such a learned presence so he thanked them both, took the crutch, and went on his way.

The ointments smelled so badly that he was forced to contain the smell by wrapping his foot in yards and yards of bandages which he purchased from his friend, the weaver. As a result, his bandaged foot would not fit into the expensive shoe that his other friend has told him to buy. He placed all the unused shoes in a pile by the door and sighed sadly whenever he saw them.

Sure enough, the pain returned when the medicine was used up and the poor man was even more miserable than he was before.

This time, he decided to go see the priest.

***

The priest listened to the man and said "We all suffer in this life, but," he continued, with great conviction, "you need not suffer alone. We will provide you with a brother-priest who will carry you."

The man blinked in disbelief. "I would prefer to walk on my own." He said.

"Nonsense," replied the priest. "We will carry you." The priest assigned a fellow priest, a large, burley man who was very strong and up to the task.

At first, it was rather nice to be carried by the big brother, and the man smiled at the people he passed in the streets from atop his broad shoulders. But after a few weeks of this treatment, the priest who had assigned the servant came to visit him in his home.

He looked very concerned as he spoke to the man, "My brother priest has reported to me that there are several places you have visited that are not, shall we say, *appropriate* for your purposes."

"What do you mean?" replied the man. "I'm only visiting those I conduct my business with. They have done no one any harm."

"Well," said the priest, "the big brother reports that only yesterday you visited the weaver."

"Yes," said the man, "he sells me my bandages."

The priest sniffed and said, "Well, he is not a member of our church and so henceforth we will not deliver you to the weaver's business." The man nodded, dumbfounded, but that was not all. The priest took a paper from his coat and unfolded it. "Here is a list of all the places that you may not go." He announced. "I trust that you will read it and comply."

The man took the letter and read it. "But this will make it impossible for me to support my family." He said. "How will we live?"

"We will provide you with a list of appropriate persons and you must have faith that that will be enough." With that, the priest got up to leave.

When the man was alone, he looked over the list and sighed. *What is to become of me and my family?* he wondered. Wishing to clear his head, he decided to go out for a walk. The big brother stood up, prepared to carry him again but the man just shook his head and waved him away. Instead, he hobbled painfully outside on his own.

***

The pain grew worse as he walked; but more than that, the man started to feel very sad. After a while, he felt so sad that he limped off the road and sat down underneath a large tree and cried.

"Why are you crying?" came a small voice from behind the tree. A little face, belonging to a young child peeked around the trunk. "What is wrong?" she said.

"Oh," said the man between sobs, "I have this pain in my foot. My wife said to ignore it but that didn't help. My friend said I needed to have better shoes, and they didn't help. The physician said I needed medicine but that didn't help. And the priest had someone carry me but really, that doesn't help much either. But, you're just a child," he said in exasperation, "I doubt you'd understand."

The child looked at the man and folded her hands while she thought. "Well, have you looked at it?"

The man's eyes went wide when he realized that he had never actually taken a look at the bottom of his foot. "Here, I have a mirror", said the child thoughtfully. "We can look together."

Seeing his foot for the first time, the man was shocked to find the end of a large, wooden splinter sticking out of a spot on his heel. With a quick tug, he removed the splinter and a wave of relief washed over him as the pain suddenly ended.

He was so happy that he took off his other shoe and tossed it into the ditch and danced around in his bare feet while the child giggled.

"And that is how your shoe got into that ditch, " said the father to his son.

"AWWW dad," said his son in disbelief, "you're just making that up!"

Antique Shoe Sign, Williamsburg VA

 **Nancy Clark Townsend** was born and raised in the Borough of Manhattan, New York City, but lived most of her life in the Lower Hudson Valley of New York State. She has always shared her home with an assortment of dogs and cats, and owned and raced several harness horses. She studied Creative Writing at Empire State College, and took courses offered by "Writer's Digest".

She has written several romance and suspense novels and is currently working on a personal memoir and an anthology of animal memoirs. She is the editor and writer for "Church Chatter" a newsletter for her church, for which she creates a Bible Word Search and Bible Acrostic. She is now retired from her work as a legal and education secretary. Nancy worked with teachers to write and produce curriculum guides for elementary and high school students. In one, she re-wrote and modernized several of Aesop's Fables.

Custom photo by Keyser Söze , used with permission

The Soccer Shoe
Nancy Clark Townsend

The young woman stopped jogging when she spied a lone black soccer shoe. How strange to see it on the paved path – as if someone simply stepped out of it and continued on their way.

Patty looked around. She saw no one nearby, which suddenly spooked her. She jogged along the Hudson River by Dyckman fields almost every evening and never worried about it. After all, she was taking Karate lessons and she carried a small can of pepper spray in her fanny pack along with her cell phone.

Tonight was a little different. She worked later than usual and hated to miss the opportunity to exercise, even though she normally jogged a bit earlier. The weather was beautiful and although it was almost eight, the sun still hovered above the Palisades. Earlier in the evening there were usually people around – some jogging or walking, some playing soccer or softball, some lounging on the benches or along the riverbank. It seemed only minutes ago that she passed a couple of joggers heading toward Dyckman Street.

Now, there was no one. Ahead of her, the path was empty. Behind her, even those other joggers were nowhere in sight. In the distance the lights of the George Washington Bridge twinkled. She could see traffic moving on both levels of the long span, but the only sounds were the muted noises of the City. They were indistinguishable, blending together like an orchestra tuning up before a performance.

The silence pressed down on her. What was she thinking? In the past two weeks there was both a rape and an attempted rape in Inwood, Manhattan Island's northernmost neighborhood. The perpetrator was as yet unidentified. Because he wore a ski mask, the women could only describe him as a large man in dark clothes. That was why Patty decided to purchase the pepper spray.

Even if she turned back now the sun would be gone by the time she reached the end of the path, and she still had the four-block walk home. The river was eerily quiet. One lone tugboat chugged northward to Albany as it pulled a long barge piled high with containers.

That solitary shoe drew her attention once again. Why would anyone leave a single shoe behind? She could understand *two* shoes, especially if they were next to the nearby bench – perhaps forgotten after a game in the player's haste to get home. But this made no sense.

She laughed softly to herself. Why did it bother her? What did it matter? Patty was a budding mystery writer, so curiosity came naturally to her. After numerous attempts, just this past week she was accepted as a client by a literary agent with an office downtown. With any luck she would soon become a published author.

Patty approached the shoe and looked down at it. It was dirty but not worn, so it was fairly new. No, it was more than dirty. There was something reddish smeared across the shoelaces. She squatted to get a closer look. Was that ... *blood*?

Suddenly, her unease turned to alarm and Patty stood up. Best to leave the shoe where it was and call the police even if they'd think she was paranoid. She turned, and a silent scream choked her. She hadn't heard him approach. Now she was staring into the dark eyes of a huge man wearing a ski mask. Had he been lurking out of sight down by the river?

Too late, she tried to unzip her fanny pack to get to the pepper spray, but he grabbed her wrists.

"I see you found my lost shoe," he said.

January Snow, photo by Betsy Riley

 **Pat Salamone** is married and lives in Florida with her husband. She has three children and several grandchildren. Pat is the author of *The Italian Thing*, which is available at Amazon.com, and the poem "Angel Dear" published in the book *Shades of Expressions.*

The Little Shoe Left in the Snow

Patricia Salamone

The dream was back. It had been years since I last had that dream. I sit on the edge of my bed with that heavy feeling. The same feeling I had as a youngster whenever I had the dream.

In my dream it is snowing; I am a child playing, tossing handfuls of snow in the air. Two boys are walking away from me. In the dream I am happy as I play, but then there is a huge darkness and I get frightened. As it looms closer to me I start to cry, then all of a sudden I am riding in either a wagon or a buckboard in the snow. I am crying, but I don't know why. I spot a small shoe laying in the snow, and that's where I always wake up with a start.

Why am I having this stupid dream again, I think. It tormented me as a child. When I told my mother about it, she told me to think about my guardian angel before I went to sleep and I wouldn't have the dream. That didn't work. One night I just stopped dreaming it. Now it was back. In the dream I am still a child, but in real life I am 40 years old and married, with three children and a full time job. We have two boys and a girl. They are happy, healthy kids, who of course love to play in the snow.

Weeks pass, I am still dreaming the dream. I tell my husband Mike about it, and how I used to dream it when I was a child. Every detail is the same. I ask him what he thinks it means.

"You are a nut," he says.

"Thanks," I say, "You're a big help."

"Look honey, you're probably just worried about the kids."

I hope he is right, but now I *am* worried about my kids. They are on my mind all day at work. I keep getting this uneasy feeling in the pit of my stomach; it is very unsettling. I am grateful my job allows me to be home before the boys arrive from school. I have a woman who watches my daughter until I get home, because she is in Kindergarten and only attends a half day.

I tell my sister about the dream; she hasn't got a clue what it means. She wants to know why I didn't tell her about it back then.

"I don't know, maybe I forgot about it during the day."

"Why don't you call Aunt Mina," Sis says, "she knows what dreams mean."

"Maybe I will," I say, and we return to our regular conversation.

Aunt Mina was my mother's oldest sister. I was twenty-eight when my mother passed away. She was the best mom in the world, but her life as a child was filled with sorrow. Grandmother died when Mom was only four years old. Grandfather died when she was sixteen, leaving her an orphan. She lived with one of her older brothers until she married my dad. She lived long enough to see my oldest son, but was gone before my other two were born. Dad passed after my second son was born. I missed them both.

More weeks pass; I am still dreaming the dream. I try to figure out why by myself. I come up with no answer. I also try to think good thoughts about my guardian angel before I go to sleep. That doesn't help either. I am getting desperate.

I finally decide to call my aunt. She is eighty-one years old and repeats herself several times during our conversation. I try to be understanding, but it is hard as I have no patience. I decide that I will go and visit her instead, since she doesn't repeat herself as much in person. I tell her I am coming on Sunday to visit. She sounds very happy about it and reminds me to bring some of the chicken and rice she loves so much.

Sunday after church, I make chicken and rice, peas and carrots, and salad. I make extra to have enough for the family too. I tell Mike that I am going to visit my aunt after dinner. I tell him I have not visited her in quite a while and that she sounded lonesome when I spoke with her earlier. Mike loved Aunt Mina, and he knew I loved her like a second Mom. He says he will take care of the home front and to have a nice visit. When I tell the kids I am going to visit Aunt Mina and Dad is going to watch them, shouts of glee and laughter erupt. I knew what that meant. They would stay up past their bed time, and have a junk food fest while I was gone.

I put the chicken and rice in a container along with some peas and carrots which I knew my aunt would enjoy. I had also baked a chocolate cake and packed enough for both of us to share with a cup of tea after her meal. Aunt Mina loved chocolate cake. I loved chocolate cake; I think the whole world loves chocolate cake. I kiss everyone goodnight (never goodbye, always 'see you later'), and tell them to behave and listen to their dad. They all but shove me out the door. Party time has started, I thought with a smile.

Aunt Mina lives in a small white house in Elmont, N.Y.; the landscaping is well maintained by some of her grandsons. When I ring the bell, she calls out, "Come in Patti, the door is open."

"Aunt Mina, why did you leave the front door open? Anyone could just walk in."

"I just opened it a little while ago after I went to the bathroom. I didn't want to have to get up again because my hip is bothering me."

"Oh, OK." I kiss her hello and she gives me a big hug and is smiling from ear to ear.

"The chicken smells good," she says.

"Do you want to eat now?" I ask.

"In a little while, I have something I want you to do for me." I knew what was coming. Aunt Mina was a beautiful woman even at the age of eighty one. She had short white hair tinted with a touch of blue. Greenish hazel eyes and a bright smile. "Patti, go downstairs and pin up the drapes that are hanging on the back wall. They are too long and I want you to pin them up so the bottom just touches the floor."

"Why?" I ask. "No one can see them anyway."

"Just do it, I know they are too long and Mary (her daughter, and my Godmother) didn't have the time. The straight pins are in the box on the table, and make sure you make it even all the way across."

"Aunt Mina," I whine.

"Just do it and shut up you little brat," she says and she starts laughing. I go downstairs and do as I was told.

When I am finished I yell up to her, "Do you want me to hem them as well?"

"No," comes the reply, "no one is going to see them anyway." I shake my head and go back upstairs. "Did you make them even?"

"Yes, Aunt Mina, I made them even."

"Good girl," she replies. "Now, how about some of that chicken and rice. And in the refrigerator is a six pack of Miller Nips; bring two of them in with you too."

"Aunt Mina! You drink beer?"

"Yes, I love my beer," she says, laughing.

"I didn't know you drank; are you becoming a wild woman, filling yourself with alcohol and running around with strange men?"

"Oh stop, you know I am not like that, I just like beer," she says, still laughing.

I heat her meal, take the two beers out of the refrigerator, and serve her on a TV tray that she has set up in front of her. After she finishes, I go into the kitchen to wash out the container.

"Patti, put the container in the cabinet above the counter," she calls out.

"Aunt Mina, this is my container from home, I was going to take it back with me."

"Well it's mine now," she says, laughing. "So just put it in the cabinet."

I open the cabinet and there are dozens of containers stacked inside. I was going to say something, but thought twice and just put the damn thing in the cabinet. I unwrap the foil from the chocolate cake, put it on a plate and slice it into two pieces.

"Oh! I smell chocolate," says my aunt.

"Yes sweetie I made a cake. I thought it would be nice to have with tea, or maybe you would rather have yours with a bottle of beer," I say, laughing.

"Stop being a brat; I will have mine with tea too," she says, laughing back at me. She finishes her meal, letting me know how delicious it was, and what a good girl I was to come see her. I clear her tray and make a cup of tea for each of us and serve it with the chocolate cake.

As we sit eating cake and drinking tea, I say, "Aunt Mina, can I ask you something?"

"What do you want to ask me?"

"Well, when I was just a kid I used to have this dream," I go on to explain the dream to her. I also tell her that I stopped having the dream when I was still a child, but now I was having it again. "Does it mean anything?" I ask. Tears start streaming down her cheeks. "Aunt Mina!

What's the matter? Why are you crying?" I think it must mean one of my kids is going to die.

"Oh, it's Flori," she says.

"Who's Flori?" I ask.

"Flori was my brother, but he died when he was six."

"What happened to him?"

"He was hard of hearing. One day he was on his way to school with my two brothers. They were walking ahead of him and he stopped to play in the snow. My brothers yelled to him that a train was coming, but he couldn't hear them, and he had his back to the train. They started running back to get him, but it was too late. The train hit him and he died instantly."

"I didn't know your brother died that young." I say.

"He was so beautiful." she says.

"Aunt Mina, don't cry. How old was my mom when he died?"

"She wasn't born at the time," she replies. "He died in 1917 and your mother was born in 1918."

"I am sorry Aunt Mina. I know this sounds silly, but what does that have to do with my dream?"

"When Flori was being buried, the family followed the hearse in a horse-drawn wagon. On the way to the cemetery we passed the spot where Flori got hit by the train. There I noticed a little shoe lying in the snow. I knew it was my brother Flori's shoe."

Chills covered my body, "What does my dream mean, then? I didn't even know him, why would I dream about that?"

"He's with you," she says.

"What do you mean? With me. In what way?"

"His spirit is in your soul. He doesn't want to be forgotten."

"Well after hearing that, I certainly will never forget him," I say.

"Good," she answers. We chat a bit more, I change the subject and soon it is time for me to leave. As I kiss my aunt goodbye, she places her hand over my heart and says, "Flori is here; love him and remember."

Another chill. "I will," I say and lock her door as I leave. On the drive home I try to put the story out of my mind, but it lingers. I feel a sense of relief when I get home. The kids are all sleeping and Mike is watching TV. I tell him what happened when I visited my aunt.

"Boy, that's weird," he says, and that is that.

***

I didn't have the dream ever again, but I never forgot about my uncle. Every once in a while he would pop into my mind.

Twenty years have passed; I am retired, and now a grandmother. My second grandson is born. As far as looks go, I think he resembles my mother's father who had one eye that drooped slightly downward. He is such a love, like all my grandchildren. I always feel a little something special for him, but cannot put my finger on it.

One day I decide to do a genealogy about my mother's family. I start out by getting copies of birth and death certificates. After weeks of filling out forms and sending money orders I receive several certificates of death from the state of New York. One of them is for my uncle Flori; as I read his date of birth, the hair on the back of my neck stands up. Flori was born September first, the same day as my second grandson.

Search Records, collage by Betsy RIley

 **Cassandra Hex** is a penname used by Betsy A. Riley for her urban fantasy stories. "Cindy Lou, Who?" appears in *Zombies Gone Wild! (vol. 1)* and "After the Plague" appeared on the (now defunct) ezine FictionAndVerse.com after winning 4th place in the 2012 NYC Midnight contest. Two novels are in final edits.

For more about Cassandra's work, and Betsy's other pennames, see BetsyARiley.com

The Goodwill Golf Shoes
Cassandra Hex

Hate came easy to Harman Wilkerson. Some would say it was inappropriate for a man of the cloth to hold such an emotion, but Harman felt he was filled with the righteous anger of the Lord. He supposed it started when his father died.

Patriarch Hamilton Wilkerson had started his career in tent revivals, parlayed that into a successful television ministry, and a massive church complex. Harman had expected that he and his brother Hubert would be brought into the ministry team and eventually inherit shares of the lucrative empire. Instead, Daddy Hamilton was exposed in a most embarrassing scandal, followed by a hurricane that leveled the massive church complex. Parishioners whispered it was the wrath of God. Hamilton took to his bed and it was rumored he was succumbing to an unsavory disease.

At the reading of the will, Harman and Hubert were surprised to learn that their father had undergone a deathbed conversion. He had left the bulk of his fortune to a rival ministry. His sons were each given a crisp twenty and instructed to buy a lottery ticket "with their father's favorite bible verse numbers."

Harman never listened that closely to his father's sermons, finding the emotional content embarrassing. He had no idea what the numbers should be. Besides, buying a lottery ticket was gambling, which he believed was a sin. He used his twenty to buy a bottle of scotch and get quietly drunk.

Hubert, on the other hand, bought a ticket with numbers that started with 3 and 16, and hit the jackpot on the multi-state lottery. Not content with riches alone, Hubert established his own evangelical empire, and pranced about on TV in a pale pink suit and a pompadour hairdo.

Harman, meanwhile, was stuck in a pious backwater town in a dry county; a position he obtained only through the charity of the man who engineered Daddy Hamilton's deathbed conversion. Once a year he received a care package from his brother Hubert. It always contained Hubert's old wardrobe, gaudy leisure garments that Harman donated to Goodwill.

The latest insult to Harman's sense of justice was the influx of refugees that the state had decided to foster. Since he was a minister, the town council expected his full support in making the new arrivals feel part of the community. Worst of all, the refugees were foreigners who purported to be Catholic.

When he first came to town, Harman had adopted the Roman collar as part of his image, mainly to distance himself from his brother. There was no Catholic church in town, but Harman looked the part of a priest more than other religious leaders in town, so most of the refugees drifted to his congregation. Harman suspected that they only adopted the guise of Catholicism to hide their secret practice of voodoo or Santeria or some other heathen religion.

The leader of the refugees was Albert Pierre, a tall dark man, who didn't even wear a proper suit to church. He wore some flowing garment that came almost to his knees, over pink-and-green-plaid pants and pink two-tone golf shoes, of all things. His very appearance offended Harman's sense of propriety, especially since he recognized the shoes and pants as ones he had donated to Goodwill.

Albert had even had the effrontery to ask Reverend Wilkerson to bless a live chicken late one afternoon. Albert had said it was for a barbeque, but Harman was sure it was for some heathen ceremony. Harman ordered a book about Haitian rituals so he would know what signs to look for. In the cemetery that adjoined the churchyard, he had already seen bowls of fruit left on graves, and candle drippings on headstones.

When Albert Pierre died suddenly, Harman was surprised that the family asked him to perform the funeral. The undertaker confided that the man was laid in his coffin barefoot, with that same flowing garment and strings of beads around his ankles. Hearing that, Harman was sure the family would have some pagan ceremony later, under cover of darkness. Not in his cemetery he vowed, and sat up night after night, watching for trespassers.

A week or so after the funeral, Harman found a new insult -- devilish items nailed to one of the trees that edged the roadway through the cemetery. There was a two-toned golf shoe, which had to be Albert's, and next to it a small doll made of crossed sticks wrapped in cloth. The book said it was called a poppet, and was used to send a message to the dead.

Harman was outraged. He pried the shoe and the poppet off the tree and stalked back to the parsonage. He threw the shoe in the trash bin back of the church, but took the poppet inside his house. He kindled a fire in the old wood stove and threw the poppet in, watching and stirring the fire with a poker to be sure it was totally consumed. He didn't bother to remove or read the strip of paper wrapped around the poppet.

Having reduced the poppet to ashes, Harman heated a can of chili and poured two fingers of scotch in a tumbler. Time was when he got invitations to dinner every night from his parishioners; sometimes he'd scored multiple invitations. Now it was only the most loyal that invited him, and only once a month or so. He wondered why.

Finishing his scotch, he debated a refill, but the level in the bottle was low and the nearest liquor store was a long drive for his rust bucket of a car. He stuck his dirty dishes in the sink to deal with later, and carefully put the scotch back in its hiding place.

He sat down to write yet another letter to his sponsor, requesting a transfer to a bigger church, or to a church in a larger town. He wrote a separate letter to his brother Hubert, asking if there might be a place for him in that organization. He sent the letters every week. He was sealing the envelopes when the kitchen door blew open.

In walked a tall, thin man, wearing a loose knee-length robe and strings of beads around his ankles. His feet were bare and left muddy footprints on Harman's floor. It was Albert Pierre.

A ghost, Harman thought, or rather a spirit -- from the scotch. It had to be his imagination. But the figure was awfully solid for either a ghost or a drunken vision. And dreams don't leave muddy footprints. And they certainly don't pull out a chair and sit down. But that's what the tall man did. Looking at Harman face to face, Albert's dark face split in a broad smile, "Good evening, Preacher," he said, "I understand you have a message for me."

Harman refused to believe in a ghost risen from the grave, and he certainly wasn't going to talk to one. He shut the kitchen door, deciding the wind must have blown it open, and went to bed.

"That's okay Preacher," the apparition called after him, "I got nothing but time. I'll just wait here till you give me my message."

Harman woke refreshed, and decided he should cut back to ONE finger of scotch, at least if he was having spicy food like chili for supper. He did his morning ablutions, dressed in his sermon clothing and walked into the kitchen. There he found Albert, or Albert's ghost, standing at the stove stirring a pan of scrambled eggs.

"Morning Preacher," Albert called out, "want some eggs?"

Harman decided to do without breakfast. He strode across to the church and sat behind the pulpit to review his notes for the sermon. When he stood up to greet the congregation before the first hymn, he noticed that the crowd was smaller. None of the refugees were there. *Good riddance*, he thought, as he introduced the first hymn.

It was during that hymn that Albert came sauntering up the aisle, his bare feet leaving muddy tracks on the worn wooden floor. He sang out loudly, and off tune before planting himself in the middle of the front pew, smack in front of Harman.

No one in the congregation seemed to notice the bizarre figure in the front pew. Albert stood for every hymn, and gyrated in an unseemly manner on the upbeat tunes. During Harman's sermon, he kept throwing up his hands and shouting "Hallelujah" or "Amen, Brother" and other shouts of praise. Each time Albert did so, Harman faltered in his speech, until at last he was so lost, he just said, "And God bless you and keep you every one," and sat down. That was the cue for the choir master to lead the recessional, and they hadn't even taken up the collection.

Harman stood at the church door, bidding farewell to the congregation and trying to ignore the pitying and puzzled looks they gave him. The whole time, Albert stood opposite him, making rude comments about the parishioners. All week Albert trailed Harman. He raided Harman's fridge, freezer, and pantry, consuming enormous amounts of food. He even made free with the last of Harman's scotch. Harman really could have used a drink, but he refused to accept the tumbler offered by the corporeal ghost.

Harman studied the little book on Haitian rituals and could find nothing about how to rid himself of the unwanted guest. By Saturday he had reached a state of desperation. He could not go through another church service like the last. He cranked up his small sedan and drove to Albert's former house to talk with the Widow Pierre. There was quite a crowd of refugees at the house when he arrived.

The Widow Pierre held court at the dining room table. In front of her sat a two-toned pink golf shoe, that had to be Albert's, and a poppet, like the one that Harman had burned.

"I am glad you have come," the widow said, "We have a problem. We sent a message to my Albert, but he did not receive it. We were telling him that we had moved to a different church," she twisted the beads around her neck. "We have seen that some of the members of your church are not comfortable with the way we express our joy during the service. Out of respect, we have moved to a church that is not as reserved. We need your help to be sure Albert gets the message this time."

Harman heaved a sigh of relief, "I would be glad to personally deliver the message to Albert. I won't even need the shoe and the poppet, I can

107

just tell him directly." As the words came out of his mouth, he realized he probably should not have let on that he could see Albert. He hurried home, told Albert of the refugees' move to a different church.

Albert said, "Thank you, Preacher," and walked out the kitchen door.

Harman got his first good night's sleep in a week and rose early. He was eager to do a good sermon to make up for last week's fiasco. But when he got to the church, he found Albert and the rest of the refugees waiting at the door. He noticed several he had not seen before, who were barefoot like Albert. More "ghosts" he supposed.

"What are you doing here?" he asked, not sure if he should address Albert or the Widow Pierre.

"Albert tells us that you can see him and talk to him directly. This is a rare talent, so we have come with all our departed to belong to your church forever." She motioned to one of the men, one wearing shoes, and he brought over a cardboard box. "We realize our presence may drive away your other parishioners, but we will make it up to you. Here is a token gift to express our appreciation," she said, fishing out a bottle of scotch for his inspection. Two more men carrying identical boxes stood in line.

Harman supposed that he might get used to the new situation. As long as he had enough bottled spirits, he could deal with the barefoot ones.

The Spirit is Willing

 A multi-award winning author, **Jeffrey B. Roth** is a well-known investigative reporter, who covers crime, law, politics, sciences, business, medicine, education, history and a wide range of other topics. In 2010, Roth won first place for a new series in the Keystone Press Awards, sponsored by the Pennsylvania Newspaper Association. A published short story writer and poet, Roth is listed in the Locus Index of Science Fiction and Fantasy Authors. Currently, Roth writes for CBS Philadelphia, CBS Baltimore, the Philadelphia Examiner and regional publications, including Carroll Magazine, Carroll Business Quarterly and Hagerstown Magazine to name a few. In the past, Roth, a former crisis intervention counselor and teacher, has written for numerous Pennsylvania newspapers, state and national magazines and the Associated Press. He lives in the foothills of the Appalachian Mountains, west of Gettysburg, PA.

A Giant Lost his Left Shoe

Jeffrey B. Roth

No one believed me nearly a century ago, when I told them a giant lost his left shoe while saving my brother from drowning; I doubt anyone would find my story any less incredible, today.

As the sun sets on my life, the intensity of that golden day and the glorious golden light of my memory has never dimmed. Nor has the sense of wonder I experienced on the day I found the large, brassy-toned shoe-like object, not far from the Sachs Mill covered bridge, south of Gettysburg, Pennsylvania. More accurately, I thought, it was part of the left foot of the giant hero who appeared in a swirling mass of smoke, blue sparks, and static electric arcs, erupting and hissing on the surface of Marsh Creek. From that day on, the place became sacred to me, and I secretly christened it Apollo's

111

Garden. I was what kids of today call a geek, then, as I am now.

It was the summer of 1917, and America had entered the Great War – the War to End All Wars, exacting a horrendous toll of life. Of course, I was barely six, and to me the war was about air aces, submarines, tanks and heroes – all the glory without any sense of real horrors of the blood-muddied trenches, mustard gas, and dysentery -- all mingled with unending explosions, screams of injured and dying horses and men, and the all-pervasive smell of death that rode the miasmic winds of a man-made Tartarus, the deepest pit of Hades.

In the dawning days of my childhood, sweet, fragrant, dazzling nature was complemented by a warm community and a loving, and I should add, tolerant and patient family. It was the antithesis to the nightmare reality of the Western Front, where the God of War, Ares, ruled. Life that day on the damp green meadow constituted my Elysian Fields – my vision of the paradise of the ancient Greek underworld ruled by Hades.

Death did not shun my world. As a thief, death appeared and disappeared in an instant, releasing an emotional wellspring, flooding a day or two with sadness, before the world righted itself, and death traveled elsewhere on its rounds. The Grim Reaper knocked twice on our door that summer – once when my beloved dog, Teddy, died after being run over by a milk truck, and the second time, Death wearing a soldier's uniform handed my father a telegram informing him that his little brother, my only uncle, had been shot down in a dogfight over No Man's Land. Forever, not to return from Flanders fields where

"*...the poppies blow*
Between the crosses, row on row,
That mark our place; and in the sky
The larks, still bravely singing, fly
Scarce heard amid the guns below."

They were the brave dead and in my innocence, I knew them not – yet did I see and not see the collector of souls that sweltering day of the 7th of July, a full four months and four days before the 11th hour of the 11th day of the 11th month silenced Germany's "Dicke Berta" known as Big Bertha by the Allies, as well as all other guns, great and small.

Lying on my back, under a darkling sky of roiling cumulonimbus giants driven into a rage by a fierce, baking sun, I watched dragon flies darting to and fro, stopping, then rising vertically, before resuming a game of tag with larger dragons pursuing, then capturing the smaller prey – what I learned a few years later was the mating dance of the dragonfly.

Quiet as a mid-afternoon, midsummer day can ever be – amidst the call of birds, some as warnings to intruders, some to their mates and some simply to sing; the small splash made by fish capturing a bug floating slowly downstream toward the dam; the plop of a large bullfrog leaping from its perch along the muddy creek bank; a dog barking in the distance; the trrrrrr... c-c-c-c of cicadas – locusts as the locals called the raucous insects.

I must have nodded off in my reveries. My last memory, before I woke to Jimmy's screams, was the prismatic flash of a rainbow refracted by a hovering dragon's wings ...

"Help. Help ... drowning ... can't ... make it ..."

Thrashing and slapping the water. Head visible, then disappearing under a frothing wake of desperation, Jimmy's voice and struggles were diminishing with each frenzied attempt he made to keep his head above water.

At first, I was unsure if I were dreaming. Jimmy's shouts mingled with nature's cacophony, not registering as pleas for help, at first, until the fog of sleep lifted.

As anyone confronted with an intense, adrenalin-pumping experience can relate, those first few seconds seemed to elongate into hours, as time slowed. Gaining control of my body, I sprang from the earth and bolted toward the bank.

"Jimmy. Hold on. Jimmy. I'm coming – hold on," I heard myself bark orders at the same time my thoughts became insistent prayers – *Don't let him drown. Please. Don't let him die. Please. Please. Please, God, please, no.*

One second he was there, struggling to maintain the surface., the next … . Gone. Only a wake and bubbles identified where he had been a short eternity before.

"Jimmy. Jimmy. Jimmy.

"No. No. No.

"Please God.

"Please God.

"Please God.

"No."

As time sped up to a frantic, impossible pace, I raced toward the bank, stripping off my shirt as I ran. Stumbling. Regaining my balance. Still wearing my brand new Keds.

Almost there. Coming. Jimmy. Jimmy. Please Jimmy. I'll save you.

Lightning erupted on the surface. Water roiled.

Zzzzz-zzt.

Hissing like an International Harvester Titan steam tractor venting pressure.

Zzzzz-zzt.

A blinding sun, hovering, dissipating the mist-steam-clouds.

Thunder.

Boom. Rumble. Boom.

Hissss.

Zzzzz-zt.

Something in the mist.

The spectacle halted my mad rush to the water.

Unbelievable.

Something. Something.

What ...?

More thunder. Blue lightning. The smell of superheated iron/copper.

Lightning. The tang of ozone.

Large. Golden. Giant.

Clank, hiss, *zzzzz-zt.*

Crackle. Crackle. Arcing blue sparks.

Hair on my arms standing upright.

Static electricity.

I stared, mouth open. A million creepy-crawlers dancing on the exposed skin of my legs, my arms, my chest, my face.

A golden arm reached deep under the surface of the water.

Eyes. Glowing blue.

Skin. Brassy-gold, streaked with soot.

Screeching, clinking, popping gears.

Deeper it reached.

Body rising above the surface, the giant's arm slowly came up, out of the water.

"Jimmy?"

Jimmy, grasped by a giant hand.

Not moving.

Sagging, limp.

"JIMMY."

Blue sparks radiating from the giant's chest.

Dancing down along its right arm.

Firing on Jimmy's chest.

Sparking.

Zzzzz-zt.

Movement.

"Jimmy."

He's moving.

Alive.

"JIMMY."

More movement.

Coughing.

Choking on water as it erupts from his mouth.

Gah ... gagging.

Coughing.

More water. More coughing. More gagging.

Stagnant seconds transmuting into racing minutes.

Floating higher. The giant. Angel. God. Apollo – it hovered five feet above the water.

Except for the clamoring clanks, clicking gears, hisses, crackling sparks – silently, slowly, it moved to the bank a bit upstream. As I stood, frozen by shock and awe of the impossible spectacle, the golden giant gently deposited Jimmy on the sweet summer grass.

It turned, focusing its shimmering, stuttering gaze on me.

I forgot to breathe.

More blue sparks. Stronger. More urgent. Growling gears. That lightning smell. Rumbling thunder. Steam hissing, shrieking. Its golden glow brightened.

I could barely look without shielding my eyes.

Then.

Then.

A pop and tremendous bang.

Gone.

No longer frozen by shock, I took a breath. Another and another. Running to Jimmy who was stirring, groaning. Coughing again.

"Jimmy?"

"Johnny, what happened?"

"Jimmy."

"Drowning. I was drowning. You saved me."

"No. Jimmy. No. Not me."

"Thank you. Thank you. I was drowning. You saved me. But how did you get me outta the creek. You're not that good of a swimmer."

Jimmy shook his head wildly, flinging water from his hair. Standing, Jimmy hopped on his left foot, while thumping the right temple with the palms of his hands; then, right foot, left temple, trying to dislodge the water trapped within the ear canals.

"You're a hero, Johnny." A grin.

Grabbing me. Hugging me. I could smell the lightning on him. In his hair, mingled with odor of summer creek -- water, mud, sand, I could smell the metal giant.

"I didn't. I mean, I would've. But I didn't. It. It. It was ... amazing. A giant. A giant appeared and plucked you from beneath the water. A giant. Not me. Golden giant."

Involuntary shivers and frissons cascaded throughout my body. Crying. I was crying.

Jimmy released me from the bear hug. Looking at me. Grinning from ear-to-ear.

"A giant? Johnny? Did you say giant?"

"Big. Golden. With electric sparks and steam. It appeared. Saved you. Disappeared. Like the Greek sun god, Apollo. You saw him? Right? You musta seen him."

"You're a hero, but instead of taking credit for saving me, you make up stories. You're a funny kid, you know that? Other kids are right. You're weird. A Jules Verne, H.G. Wells, science fiction, Greek myth crazy person – but I love ya, little brother."

"You had to see him. Jimmy. He was real. He saved you. Not me."

With a wink, a chuckle and a muss of my hair, Jimmy smiled. Shaking his head.

"You're something kid. Really something ... ." As if struck by static electricity, Jimmy flinched, before saying: "Don't tell Ma and Pa or they'll never let us come here by ourselves again. Promise you won't tell."

"But Jimmy ... "

"Promise. Cross your heart and hope to die. Stick a needle in your eye. Promise. Swear."

Jimmy was wearing his you-better-do-it-or-you'll-be-sorry look.

"Swear!"

No arguing with that look.

"I promise I won't tell Ma or Pa."

"Or anyone else. Got it kid? No one. Understand?"

"Got it."

"Say it."

"What?"

"Swear."

"Cross my heart and hope to die, stick a needle in my eye. I swear."

Another gentle muss of my hair, and he got up; walked over to collect his clothes and shoes, which were lying near the bank. Put on his shoes. Squish, squish, with each step until his feet dried on the half-hour walk home. Afternoon chores to do.

"Remember kid. Not a word."

I nodded, pledging obedience to his decree.

He went to the barn to muck manure and grab some straw bales to spread in the giant Belgians' stalls. I went to the wellhead pump to fill buckets to water the animals. Pa was in town, picking up supplies at Klinefelter's Feed and Grain Store, getting a haircut, and chewing over the news of the day with the other farmers who congregated around the pickle barrel on Wednesday afternoons.

As the day progressed, the thunderclouds rose to extreme heights, forming cotton-white mountains with cliffs, summits, and plateaus. Turning gray, then nearly black beneath, they was a sure sign of a July storm on the march.

The animals. restless, agitated, sensed the thunder and lightning to come. The air died. Hardly a breeze. The temperature rose sending the mercury up near 100.

When they came, the storms promised to kick up quite a ruckus. The smell of sweet rain and lightning was in the air.

The golden orb of the summer sun flashed as it came out from behind a cloud, and my mind jumped back to the golden giant. I promised I wouldn't tell, and I planned to keep that promise. They'd all just laugh and say I had my head in the clouds as usual. But I knew it was real. I knew.

Pa got home just as Jimmy and I were finishing our chores and we were heading inside for supper. Ma had been cooking and baking all day. My mouth watered as soon as I opened the screen door and stepped across the threshold. The sweet scent of freshly-baked bread, and the aromas of broiled beef, boiled potatoes, candied-carrots, savory gravy, and fresh rhubarb pie greeted me.

The kitchen, itself, an oven, but somehow Ma didn't looked frazzled or fried, as she hummed and darted from stove, to table, to sink, to cupboard; then back to the stove, where she retrieved a bright copper teakettle that was furiously steaming, its whistle mutating into a ear-piercing shriek. Rays from the sun glinted off the dangling bits of glass adorning the fancy crystal lamp Pa had got for Ma's birthday, sending flashing rainbows across the surfaces of the kitchen.

The golden giant. I wanted to tell, to scream. I was bursting with the secret, but I promised and I wouldn't. Jimmy would be mad. Ma and Pa wouldn't believe it anyway. Except for God in Heaven, they believed only what they could see with their own eyes, touch with their own hands, hear with their own ears. A daydream, they'd say.

Ma pointed at me and Jimmy.

"John Herbert Wells, how'd you get so dirty?"

"I was …"

"Never mind, you'll just tell me one of your stories. Go get washed-up," her Pennsylvania Dutch accent so thick it sounded like warshed-up. "Get a move on and get it done. Then Johnny, you can help set the table. Jimmy, you get to warsh dishes. It's your turn tonight."

Rainbows painted her flour-dusted apron and shimmered across her arms. Pans clanked. Dishes clinked. More rainbows blossomed, as I headed upstairs to *warsh-up*.

The giant. I saw it. I know I saw it.

By the time I returned to the kitchen, Pa and Jimmy were in their seats, waiting for me to finish my ablutions and take my place at the large pine table, while Ma stood like a guard, waiting for one of us to make a wrong move.

"Hands, please," Ma demanded. "Now the other side."

A daily ritual. So commonplace, it acted to ease the discordance of the fantastic I had experienced. A counterpoint of normality and sanity.

"Jimmy. Your turn to say grace," Ma reminded him.

We ate. Dishes were *warshed* and put away. Pa went out on the porch to puff on his pipe. Ma sat beside Pa on the porch swing, humming, while she worked on a quilt.

Cicadas trilled. Flies buzzed. Thunder rolled toward us. Lightning flashed at a distance. The smell of a summer storm infused the strengthening gusts as colossal clouds came bearing down on our farm.

The golden giant.

Amidst a mesmerizing clash of light and darkness, howling winds, shutters rattling, I sat on my bed and watched the gods battle each other for the power of Mt. Olympus. I imagined the golden giant leading the assault, armed with lightning bolts stolen from the arsenal of Zeus.

As the storm retreated, I slid into a deep sleep. Dreams of heroes. Dreams of warriors. Of giants. Of gods. Of miracles. Of the impossible.

My giant active in each scenario. Materializing, lightning lancing the sky. My giant was there, whispering to me: "I'm real."

Storm after storm trod through the real world as army after army passed through my dreams. War machines rumbled. Cannon fired. Bolts of lightning exploded in the heavens.

Usually, I didn't remember much of my dreams. Only vague, incongruous fragments, really.

Not so the morning after my giant appeared. I remembered every detail about the rescue of my brother.

"In the field," the giant said. "Go back to the creek and search the field. I'm there."

Itching to escape the farm and search for evidence to prove my story, I rushed through my chores – fed the chickens, slopped the hogs, fed the horses and cows. In my haste, I nearly forgot to collect the eggs for Ma.

She spied me getting ready to scamper away, when she called.

"Johnny. Where's them eggs?"

Back to the hen house I ran. Snatching up the eggs, I fast-footed the clutch of warm brown eggs to the kitchen and delivered the bounty.

Ma smiled at my back as I rocketed through the screen door. It slammed shut.

"How many times do I have to tell ya? Don't slam that dang door."

By then I was halfway down the lane, heading for the dirt road that wound its way to the bridge. Along the way, yellow and white cabbage butterflies circled puddles of water deposited during the night's heavy downpour. As I neared the creek, dragon flies began crossing my path – darting here and there.

Since the giant said check the field, I reckoned that I should use the place he appeared as my base camp, and then search in a widening arc from that point. An hour whizzed by with the speed of a dragonfly. Then another and another, as I continued to examine each square inch of the fallow ground for the proof that the giant assured me was there.

"Eureka," I shouted aloud.

As did Archimedes, I held the treasure I had found above my head and ran through the field, leaping and dancing and shouting. Not as golden, as I remembered. More soot, tarnish and scratches; nicked and dented, but it was real.

When I had regained control of my excitement, I carried my find to side of the creek, about the same place I had been when the giant materialized. I studied every facet of the object, taking a break in the examination to look out over the creek to the spot where it had first appeared.

Time flew, yet seemed to stand still. Before I knew it, the morning had metamorphosed into afternoon, then evening crawled out from its chrysalis.

After hours of debating its function, I decided it was a small portion of toe of the giant's left shoe – a very small portion. Not much more than a bit of curved brass. Smooth on the exterior, except for scars and other small defects.

Its innards intrigued me the most. Vein-like lines ran in a fern frond pattern from a central point branching out to all points. Each vein appeared to contain a hair's-width thin wire of some kind – so small as to make me wonder whether I was actually seeing the fiber or whether it was a concoction of my imagination.

Proof. I had proof.

Now Jimmy had to believe me.

Artifact in hand, I ran until my lungs threatened to explode. Hating the fact that I had to stop to catch my wind, I'd sprint even faster when my marathon continued.

My trip home was about 5 miles, not the 26.2 miles that the Athenian herald, Pheidippides, ran from the Marathon battlefield, in 490 BC.

After arriving in Athens to announce the Greek victory, he dropped dead. At times, I felt as if I were about to mimic Pheidippides and drop dead upon reaching our farm lane.

A gallon of water later, I made it through the screen door to the kitchen, with my precious find tucked safely in my back pocket. Between more gulps of water and sharp intakes of breath I managed to croak words.

"Ma ... Jimmy ... where ... Jimmy?"

"Take a breath and calm down boy. You're all in a lather. I declare you're more heated than Pa's old pipe. For land's sake, I'm guessing he's down to the McDaniel's to see their girl – whatshername ... Lizzie. He's getting smitten with her. What's lit a fire under you?"

"Nothing Ma. I just wanna show him something."

"He'll be back by chore time. In the meanwhile, get yourself upstairs and change those sweat-soaked clothes so I can warsh them. Speaking of warsh, you should grab a warsh rag and clean the dust and dirt off your arms, legs and face. You look like you been rolling it a dirt pile. Get up them stairs and warsh. Chore time's a coming up."

Knowing a response other than "yes Ma'am," wouldn't be greeted with a smile – Ma hated backtalk – I did as told.

I knew I should take the giant's toe and put it in my secret hidey-hole for safe keeping, but I was loathe to leave it out of my sight, afraid it might vanish like the rest of its owner. Better safe than sorry, I decided.

I grabbed a clean sock and put the toe into the toe. I moved my bed about a foot to the right and pried up the loose floor boards to uncover my treasure trove of train spikes, trinkets and other jewels beloved by young boys. Placing it with care, directly in the middle of my hoard, I hesitated before releasing my grip on the prize.

Floorboards in place, bed back to its place, I changed clothes and cleaned up. When I returned to the kitchen, I almost ran into Pa as he headed toward the stairs – also under orders from Ma to "warsh up."

I went outside to the porch swing with a pad and pencil to draw, while I kept watch for Jimmy heading down the lane. My plan was to wait until after supper, then show him proof that it wasn't all in my head.

During the several hours I waited for my errant brother to return, I started each sketch with a drawing of the toe I had found. Each time, I expanded the drawing until I had a version of the giant I remembered.

Each drawing became more and more detailed. It wasn't long before I began to draw what I imagined to be interior views of the mechanism – for I was sure, even then, that what I had saw was an automaton, a mechanical man.

It had to be a machine because of the steam, the sparks, the sounds it made, the way it moved, and, of course, because it was made of metal, not flesh and blood. And machines had gears, pulleys, pistons and other parts that worked together to allow the apparatus to perform its function.

My first drawings looked like Tik-Tok from *The Road to Oz*, which I just finished reading the month before. Later drawings resembled the Iron Giant from *Ozma of Oz*.

Time dilated again, as I counted seconds and minutes, charting the shadow of the sun as it journeyed toward the western horizon. The more I willed Jimmy to appear, the more I became frustrated as day turned to twilight.

Jimmy is gonna get it for this. Ma will tan his hide if he misses his supper.

Perhaps it was the gentle rocking of the porch swing, or the warming rays of the sun – both conspired to lure me back into the kingdom of dreams. Next thing I remember was the kitchen door slamming home and Ma's mantra.

"Jimmy, would you please stop slamming that door? Next thing it will be off its hinges."

"Sorry Ma."

"Get upstairs and warsh and get back down here."

"Yes, Ma'am."

Before I could catch him, Jimmy had taken the steps two-at-a-time and had barricaded himself in the bathroom. I followed, approaching the door with apprehension.

I tapped.

"I'm in here. Wait and I'll be out."

"Jimmy," I said, as I tapped again.

"Geez, if you can't wait use the outhouse for the love of Pete."

I winced at the expression. If Ma heard him, she'd have lye soap in his mouth before he could spit.

"Jimmy, I found it."

"Found what?"

"Proof."

"Of what?"

"That the golden giant really was there and really did save you from drowning."

"Keep it down or Ma may hear you. If I get in trouble, you'll get it double from me."

"You have to see it. Please – only take a minute or two."

"If I say yes, we'll you let me finish my business in peace?"

"Yes. I promise. Just come to our room when you're done."

"Fine. Anything to get a little privacy."

Reluctantly, I walked down the hall to our bedroom on the left. I hesitated going away from the door, fearing Jimmy would sneak out the bathroom and barrel downstairs instead of keeping to his word.

With one last glance at the closed bathroom door, I darted inside and as quietly as possible, pushed my bed to the side, carefully pried up the floorboards. A wave of relief washed over me when I saw the bulge in my old sock, knowing the proof had not vanished; nor had it been a figment of my imagination.

With treasure in hand, I rolled the sock open, revealing the object that would prove to Jimmy that it was the giant and not me, who saved him from drowning. A ray from the westering sun glanced off the scratched and scored medal hinting at a rainbow.

Curiously, the object seemed less brilliantly gold to me now. Perhaps the passage of time diminished my awe of the object I first found and the one I now held in my hands. Amazing still. This was proof beyond doubt.

"So what are you so riled up about that couldn't wait till I was out of the bathroom?" Jimmy said as he walked into the room.

Startled out of my reveries, I closed the sock over my proof. I wanted to explain my theories about the events at the creek, in a dramatic way, so Jimmy would understand how I reached the conclusions I had drawn about my giant.

"What ya got there kiddo," Jimmy said as he came up in front of me.

Looking up at him towering over me, I had a vision of the giant holding Jimmy in one hand. The impossible immensity of the entire event settled over me and added to my fear that no matter what evidence I had, no matter how convincingly I related the event, people would still relegate the tale to just that – one of Johnny's fantastic stories.

"Well," Jimmy urged, as he stood looking down at me, tapping his right foot, arms crossed as if to ward off anything I might say. "I'm waiting."

Nearly frozen by anxiety, I looked at my big brother. My voice quaked, quivered and squealed.

"Here," I said holding the sock and its content up to him like a subject presenting a boon to his lord. "It's ... I mean ... It's proof that a giant saved you, not me."

Words tumbling out like a clumsy clown with two left feet, I felt faith in my proof flee and my conviction that what I saw actually happened crumble. Nothing that occurred in my brief life had been so important to me as having Jimmy accept my story as an accurate account of what happened that summer afternoon.

Jimmy took the sock; held the toe with his right thumb and index finger; inverted it; and dumped the object into his left hand. Tossing the sock in my face, with a chuckle and a grin, he turned the piece of battered metal for a cursory examination.

"So ... so what's this supposed to be?" Jimmy stopped looking at the metal that now seemed darker and less golden than at any time I had gazed at it in wonder. He tossed it into the air from hand-to-hand as if it were a ball to be juggled. "Well?"

"A toe."

"A what?"

"A toe ... part of the shoe the giant lost when he disappeared and went back to where he had come from in the first place."

"A giant's toe or maybe his shoe?"

"Please, look at it again. This time really look at it."

As each second seeped into the next in a sluggish train of time struggling to get to the next second on the line, I felt my body, my essence, everything that defined me, shrink inward. I felt smaller and smaller, as Jimmy grew larger and taller.

"It's a piece of some kind of brass. Hard to say what it came from."

Tossing it higher each time, Jimmy shook his head.

"Another piece of junk, just like other junk you collect and put in your secret hiding place under the bed."

Jimmy knows about my secret place and my secret things stored there.

"Don't look so surprised. I've always known where you hid stuff. When this was just my room, before you showed up, I used to hide my stuff there. Pa told me once, that when he was young, he used to hide his stuff there, too. Sorry pal, not much of a secret."

Fear turned into rage. Trickling time became a flood. Sanity, insanity. As if I were being launched into the sky on a rocket, before the next second knew its place, I was off the bed, grasping to catch my "junk" before gravity returned it to Jimmy's waiting palm.

The momentum of the force I employed in my leap nearly knocked Jimmy on his behind. Shock, surprise, then anger danced across his face.

Before he could react or say another word, I had recovered the object, recovered my balance and ran out of the room in an attempt to recover my dignity. Jimmy's words and reaction barely registered with me as I exploded down the hallway; jumped, rather than ran, down the staircase; made a beeline for the front door which no one but guests ever used; flung the heavy oak door open; and with nary a thought of closing it behind me, out of the house I flew.

By the time my sanity and sense of self returned, I found myself in a frantic flight down the road leading to the covered bridge. Sides aching, breathless, dizzy with exhaustion, shame and anger, my pace slowed.

Dragons chased each other. Frogs and cicadas beckoned. Without conscious will, as if sleepwalking through molasses, inexorably, I was drawn to the spot along the bank where I had witnessed the giant.

Legs collapsing under me, my bottom found earth. A sharp pain focused my attention to my right hand. Instinctively, I had been gripping the object with such strength that its sharp edges had cut deep into my flesh, causing blood to run in crimson rivulets over the surface of the object, then drip on my pants.

Tears came unbidden. Fluctuating between anger at betrayal, and shame for stupidity, I nearly flung the dirty, dull piece of brassy-junk into the middle of the stream, where it could rust and rot for eternity.

For some reason, I resisted the impulse and released my stranglehold on the lump of metal. Maybe it was the pain that brought me back to my senses. The pain was as real as the metal I was holding. It was real. The giant was real. I knew beyond any sense of doubt, I was right.

Never again did I mention the giant to a single soul. Clearly, no one would believe me.

Despite Jimmy's occasional taunts about the "golden giant" and my "fanciful yarns," my belief in the reality of my experience never faltered. I found a secret place – one that no one would ever find -- to hide my treasure.

Obsession about the nature of the object and its fantastic origins never diminished. Surreptitiously, I would vanish from the house for an hour or two, retrieve the bit of metal and examine it with a magnifying glass I had bought for that purpose at Lane's Pharmacy, with money I had saved from my allowance for doing chores.

Through the intervening years, I filled notebooks with drawings of the object, along with theories of the giant's origins. In the summer of 1918, while people were getting sick and dying of the Spanish Influenza, I contracted polio. Old Doc Sterner did not figure out why I felt increasingly weak that year.

Later, when I got worse, and had trouble walking and doing chores, Ma and Pa loaded me up in Mr. Klinefelter's new Monroe Coupe and drove for six hours to the hospital in York – a drive that today takes about an hour. Dr. Rheinhardt, a patient, tall man, with a thick German accent, confirmed my parents' worst fears when he told them I had infantile paralysis.

Ma cried, telling the doctor that she had warned Jimmy and I about swimming in the creek during the dog days of summer. Dr. Rheinhardt listened and tried to explain that the disease was caused by the poliovirus, discovered eight years before by another doctor with a German-sounding name.

Pa, always stoic when faced with any expression of emotion on the part of others, listened and nodded. It was the way of the Pennsylvania Germans – never react to news good or bad; and, above all, don't tempt fate by telling others about having any good luck.

The disease did not cripple me, but it left me with a right leg that was slightly smaller than my left leg. During the next year, my condition improved. Of course Ma viewed any hint of lethargy I displayed as a sign that my health was drastically deteriorating.

Ma made Pa move Jimmy's bed to the attic room as a precaution – fearing he might catch the polio. Most of the time, Jimmy avoided me, until Ma forced him to entertain me for an hour or two. His reticence about spending time with me was due more to his age of 14 and his increased fascination with Lizzie, than fear of falling prey to my disease.

Polio was considered a curse, one of the worst things which could happen to a child. Ironically, for me, it was a blessing of sorts. For the first time in my life, I was afforded a level of privacy I had never before experienced. Another benefit was that Ma, Pa, relatives and friends of the family, all knew I was a voracious reader.

My convalescence swam with books – *Tom Swift and His Air Glider*, Tom *Swift and His Aerial Warship*, *Tom Swift In the Land of Wonders*, *Bulfinch's Mythology: The Age of Fable*; *The Age of Chivalry*; *The Age of Charlemagne*; *The Princess of Mars*, and the Tarzan books of Edgar Rice Burroughs; books on history, science and even some tomes of classical Greek philosophy – Plato and Aristotle.

By the time I was allowed to return to school, I had amassed a rather large knowledge of literature, history and the sciences. Before polio, I had been a lackluster, less than enthusiastic student; but upon my return to school, I excelled, getting the highest grades in all of my courses. In fact, I often did better in my subjects than did students in the eighth grade – the year most students, especially the boys, quit school to work full-time on the farms.

It wasn't long before I had accumulated a number of academic awards. My scholastic prowess garnered the attention of the school board president – Dr. Gladfelter, a professor of mathematics and physics at Pennsylvania College, in Gettysburg.

Throughout those years, I continued my study and speculations about the artifact and the scientific wonders it represented. In my readings, and at school, I first heard about the special and general theories of relativity postulated by Albert Einstein. At one of the school award dinners presided over by Dr. Gladfelter, I had a chance to ask him about some details of those theories.

Apparently, my fervor for science, and especially, mathematics, in addition to my queries about relativity, convinced Dr. Gladfelter I was worthy of cultivation. Unexpectedly, on the Monday after I had been awarded a ribbon for being the best student in mathematics, Dr. Gladfelter dropped by with books on physics.

That afternoon, after I accepted the gift and thanked him, he asked to speak privately to Ma and

Pa. Jimmy had used the professor's visit as an opportunity to beat feet to Lizzie's farm. With the books, in hand, I was exiled to my room – Ma still worried about me being in the outside air too long at a time.

Dr. Gladfelter continued to visit me over the years. First spending some time with me talking about mathematics or the latest discoveries in science; then spending some time talking to my parents after I had been banished from the parlor.

That all changed when I graduated from the eighth grade.

Dr. Gladfelter appeared at our door on a Saturday evening. All that day, Ma had been cleaning, cooking and ordering Pa and Jimmy around, doing special chores as if one of the relatives were coming for a visit.

By later afternoon, Ma told me to go upstairs to take a bath and then put on my Sunday church clothes. Pa and Jimmy were given the same marching orders.

When I came down, Ma made me stand in front of her for a close inspection. Sensing nervous excitement emanating from her as she checked behind my ears, my fingernails and insuring the part of my hair was straight, I wanted to ask her what all the fuss was about, but I didn't.

Ma was the type of person who could not be rushed into anything. Every choice she made was done according to her own highly specific rationales and timetables. When and if she were ready, she would share what was causing her to be so fidgety and flustered.

Pa and Jimmy joined us in the parlor. The dining room was decked out with holiday formality – the good silver; Grandma's china, which Ma had inherited; a clean and smartly ironed table cloth – all indications that something or someone of great importance was coming to dinner.

"Now be on your best behavior. All of you; and that includes you Pa, and especially you, Jimmy."

"Yes, Ma'am," they both chimed.

Outside, Max, the mixed-shepherd dog that Lizzie had given us from a winter litter, began announcing the arrival of visitors. Soon Max's yelps were joined by the putt-putt of a car engine coming closer to the house. The car stopped, the engine sputtered to a stop, doors opened and shut, and shortly, footsteps mounted the front porch, approached the door and a loud rap heralded the arrival of the guests.

Pa stepped forward, opened the door and greeted Dr. Gladfelter, Mr. James, our school teacher, and a stranger, who was dressed in a black suit, pressed white shirt with a black tie, who held a brief bag.

"Mr. and Mrs. Wells, let me introduce Dean Arthur Schumucker, president of Pennsylvania College."

After a flurry of introductions between adults, Jimmy, then I were the last to be recognized.

"Hello Johnny. It's such a pleasure to meet you. Dr. Gladfelter and your teacher, Mr. James, have told me so much about you that I feel that I already know you."

Without relating all that happened that remarkable evening, the short of it was that I was being accepted at a private-boarding school, a college preparatory academy, located near Lancaster. All my tuition and expenses were being paid to send me to school, with the expectation that when I graduated 12th grade, I would apply and be admitted to Pennsylvania College on a full scholarship.

Speechless does not do any justice to the depth of silence and sense of unreality that seized my being that night. At the end of August, I would take the train to Lancaster and begin a new life of academics.

August arrived at the speed of light. After a week or so becoming acclimated to my new surroundings, and months of being razzed for being the poor son of a dirt farmer, I found my pace and excelled in everything academic. The four years sped by.

That September, I found myself in a boarding house in Gettysburg, where Mrs. Rice let rooms to college students. On weekends, I visited Ma and Pa. By then, Pa had managed to buy an adjacent 55-acre-farm, which he gave to Jimmy and his wife, Lizzie, who now had two tow-headed kids, David and Henry.

College passed in what now seems an instant. Again, I had out-performed all the students in my class, and was named class valedictorian. Dr. Gladfelter, during those four years, acted as my mentor and adviser, helping set my path to the University of Pennsylvania in Philadelphia, where I earned a Masters of Science, in physics, and later, a Ph.D., in physics and mathematics.

World War II had entered the timeline. All men of draft age were expected to do their duty. I wanted to enlist, but my bout with polio quickly ended any dreams I may have had of serving my country in the military.

I may have been 4F as far as the military was concerned, but the War Department had no compunctions about recruiting me to work with other scientists tasked with helping America to win the war. Briefly, I did a stint at Los Alamos and worked with Oppenheimer and Teller on the country's secret weapon, the atomic bomb. I even met Einstein. Following the war, I went back to academia and research at the university.

Despite the fact I had long ago put away childish things, my examinations of the relic of my youth never waned. In fact, the opposite was true – I became completely obsessed with the giant's left toe.

I'm not sure when I first realized that it was vitally important for me to solve the mystery of the golden giant. I knew only that solve the riddle I must, or face a world radically changed from the one I now knew. It started as a hunch, which turned into simple speculation, which evolved into a theory, then an epiphany, and finally another eureka moment.

That was five years ago.

All of my life, I knew that if the golden giant had never saved Jimmy, had never appeared to me, had never left behind a puzzle, everything would be drastically different. Without it, Jimmy would have been decades dead, and I, no doubt, would have been a dirt farmer, scraping by year-after-year.

Again I heard the giant's whisper, but this time it did not say *find me*, it said *create me, so then and now can be*. Without then, there could be no future become present. Each second, each minute, each hour, each day, each week, each month, each year, each decade rested on a foundation of time.

Time purposefully constructed a path leading from now back to then and the creek beside the covered bridge. I set to work to create the past.

Sun glinting off the churning, splashing water below me, I maneuvered my giant over the creek, I saw the young boy on the bank rousing from a late afternoon nap. The older boy was losing his battle in the water and had gone under for what surely was the last time.

With lightning erupting, encircling the armor of my golden giant, I reached down and grasped the lad. As if following a script, I gave the limp body several low amperage jolts of electricity.

Blue sparks radiating from the giant's chest.

Dancing down along its right arm.

Firing on Jimmy's chest.

Sparking.

Zzzzz-zt.

Movement.

After a few seconds, water spouted out of his mouth and the boy began to move. His eyes remained closed, as he coughed and gagged, each time drawing in life-giving breaths.

Traveling downstream a few yards, I piloted my machine over the spot on the bank where I had set down Jimmy all those years ago – now.

As I began to ascend into the air, I turned toward the awestruck child standing on the bank. With a flash of blue light in his direction, my giant and I rose higher, traveling above the field adjacent to the creek.

One last duty to perform before I journeyed the 80-plus years home. With the flick of a switch, a small piece of the giant's left foot – the toe, separated and fell to the ground.

More blue sparks. Stronger. More urgent. Growling gears. Lightning smell. Rumbling thunder. Steam hissing, shrieking. Its golden glow brightened.

As I disappeared in a clap of thunder and blinding flash of golden light, I knew all was right with the past, the present and the future.